ALEX CAGE
CLEAN FAST-PACED ACTION THRILLERS

# JOIN THE READER'S LIST

Get the latest releases and exclusive giveaways - sign up to
the Alex Cage Reader List:

www.AlexCage.com/signup

# ALSO BY ALEX CAGE

**Leroy Silver Series**

Contracts & Bullets

Aloha & Bullets

Politics Thieves & Bullets

**Orlando Black Series**

Carolina Dance

Bayside Boom

Bet on Black

Get the latest releases and exclusive giveaways, sign up to the Alex Cage Reader List.

www.AlexCage.com/signup

# CONTRACTS & BULLETS

## A LEROY SILVER ADVENTURE

### ALEX CAGE

## CHAPTER ONE

LEROY SILVER'S ORDERS were simple enough; take out the war criminal turned businessman by any means necessary. His superior officer provided him with the complete dossier on James Tyson. It contained everything needed for the job, from his military career to when he left the army and began supplying weapons and ammunition to shady organizations.

Silver spent a few days prepping for the assignment. It didn't take long to familiarize himself with Tyson's habits and movements. Most times, armed bodyguards, ex-military men and women, guarded Tyson. It was impossible to find him unprotected.

Neutralizing him at his home was out of the question since his estate was heavily guarded. Armed sentries patrolled the compound every moment of the day, and cameras were everywhere. It made sense for Tyson to be cautious in his line of work, given his history and the enemies he created. But it made killing him more difficult.

The kill order stated to assassinate Tyson at his daughter's high school graduation ceremony. Silver's superiors decided it was the perfect opportunity. It was at a small town outside of Portland, Oregon, the security was lax, and Tyson probably didn't expect anyone to risk the lives of children to attack him.

Silver didn't approve of the plan, but since it was government sanctioned, he went along with it. Gaining access to the school wasn't much of a problem. He broke into the campus a couple of days earlier and stashed his weapons bag inside a bathroom stall ceiling. He then wore a sports jacket and jeans to sneak into the school along with the proud families of the graduating students. The only hurdle Silver faced earlier was finding the perfect vantage point—somewhere hidden from the security cameras. He settled for the gymnasium roof. It offered a view over the field where the ceremony was, and it was near where he parked his car. He kept low and removed the rifle stock and the barrel-and-bolt assembly from his bag before connecting the two parts with an Allen wrench. Reaching back into the bag, he removed a scope and a suppressor. He attached the suppressor to the muzzle, flipped the bipod under the barrel, and rested the butt of the stock on the roof floor. After mounting the scope and adjusting for eye relief, he lay in wait. Tyson arrived just moments after the ceremony started. He wore a charcoal suit, his brown hair slicked back with gray showing at the sideburns, and two guards flanked either side of him.

Orders came specifying Silver make a headshot since it was possible for Tyson to wear a bulletproof vest under his suit. If Silver missed, he wouldn't get another chance at taking his target out again since Tyson's security would more than likely triple. Watching the principal hand out diplomas to excited kids, Silver's gut tightened, and his breath briefly filled his lungs. He had a clean shot of Tyson sitting in the front row bleachers.

Now, James Tyson was a terrible person—responsible for thousands of deaths. Silver knew assassinating the war criminal was necessary to prevent more deaths. To him, killing Tyson was easy, but not in front of his family. Silver didn't want to put them through such trauma, knowing first-hand how such things could destroy a child's future. When the principal handed out the last diploma, and the parents stood to congratulate their kids, Silver knew he missed his window; and he was okay with it. For all his flaws and evil deeds, at that moment, James Tyson was just a proud father —happy to see his kid graduate high school. Killing him in front of his family would have been despicable.

*This will ruffle some feathers*, Silver thought while packing his stuff.

As soon as he vacated the school, Silver's phone started buzzing. He already knew who it was and had been expecting the call. He waited until he was inside his car and driving away from the scene before answering it.

"Was the mission successful?" the voice asked as soon as he picked up.

"Negative, there was a complication," Silver replied.

The line went silent for a couple of moments, and he wondered if the other man had dropped the call.

"Report back to HQ now," the voice commanded.

"Roger that," Silver replied before the line went dead. He knew the government would be less than thrilled about his failure to complete the assignment.

The next morning Silver flew into LaGuardia Airport. Alone in first-class, he was first to exit the plane. The airport was noisy and crowded as he passed through and outside to ground transportation. He found an empty taxi queue, waved down a cab, and ducked in the back seat. The aroma of a sausage and egg sandwich hit his nose. He watched as the driver wiped the crumbs from his mouth.

"Where to?" the cabbie asked, still chewing.

Silver gave him the address and spent the next thirty minutes listening to the man talk about his newborn child and how great New York City was. The driver stopped at a park in Lower Manhattan, and Silver paid him before sliding out of the car. He waited until the cab left before walking across the street to a twenty-plus-story concrete structure. The building, set off to itself, was a dirty gray color and surrounded by a four-foot-tall cement wall. The only way in was through a gate next to a security hut. He approached the entrance, and a guard stepped out of the hut, holding a Heckler & Koch HK assault rifle. Silver flashed his badge and handed it to the armed man.

"One moment, sir," the man said, holding the badge to the guardhouse window.

Another guard inside the hut scanned the badge using a small electronic device before dropping his head in front of a computer screen, then peeking up at Silver every few seconds as if he were confirming his physical attributes. After fifteen seconds, he nodded to his partner and the armed guard handed Silver back the badge.

"Thank you, sir. You can go in."

Silver nodded, and as he walked toward the entrance, the gate slid apart.

Inside were unmarked vehicles and more armed patrols. Another guard checked Silver's badge at the front door. After he cleared the bomb-sniffing dogs, an explosive trace detector, and a metal detector, another guard checked one last time.

Silver took the elevator up to his superior's, that was, his handler's office. He hesitated before knocking on the door. When called inside, he opened it and entered. Seated behind a desk in a tailored, slate-blue suit was Captain Matt Anderson. He was looking down at a notepad, writing. The office was practically empty, save for the desk, chairs, and potted plant on the windowsill. Anderson's office had looked the same since Silver first started reporting to him. You'd think he started using the office only recently since there weren't any personal effects in sight, not even a picture of his family. Captain Matt Anderson had been Silver's handler ever since he got assigned to the arm of the government responsible for fixing the country's messes. Silver worked for a secret unit that very few people knew existed. Their job was to eliminate some of the world's most dangerous and influential people, preventing them from risking or taking the lives of the country's citizens. After they recruited Silver from the army, Captain Anderson took him under his wings. He was one of the few people Silver could call a friend.

Anderson looked above the bridge of his reading glasses at Silver. "Take a seat," he said as soon as Silver shut the door behind himself.

Silver settled into the chair opposite of his superior's desk. "This has to be the best view in the building," he said, looking at the window.

Anderson removed his glasses and brushed his hand through his short dirty blond hair. "So, explain to me why the target is still very much alive," he asked, sighing at the end of his question.

"I couldn't bring myself to take the shot," Silver answered, still looking in the window's direction. "Way too many civilians on the premises," he finished, turning to Anderson.

"You've taken out several targets before in sizeable crowds without endangering the lives of the civilians in proximity," Anderson pointed out. "Why was this any different?" he asked.

"Maybe it's because I was supposed to kill a man at his daughter's high school graduation?" Silver replied. "It just didn't sit right with me."

"It's the job you signed up for. How you feel about the situation shouldn't prevent you from completing your assignment. The higher-ups won't be happy when they hear about this."

"Of course, they won't," Silver sighed. "But I'm pretty sure they can find someone else who wouldn't mind blowing off Tyson's head in front of his family. Unfortunately for them, that person just isn't me," he concluded, shaking his head.

"Leroy, do you know how hard it was to get that particular intel about Tyson?" Anderson asked. "You just blew the best chance the government had of eliminating the country's most notorious war criminal."

"Come on," Silver said in an exasperated tone. "How was I supposed to blow a hole in the guy's head while his daughter was being handed her certificate?" He got up from his chair and started pacing the office. "That's just cruel— even for this agency. The kid would've been in therapy all her life. Imagine having to relive that moment every single day. It would be better if I neutralize Tyson privately—away from his family."

"I agree with the situation not being ideal," Anderson stated. "I know that, but this was the best shot we had in a long time. Tyson leaves for his private island tomorrow, and no one can get to him there. If you think his house is Fort Knox, the island is ten times more secure. His family would have recovered, eventually. Everyone has trauma they're dealing with. They wouldn't be the first."

"We're supposed to protect the lives of civilians," Silver insisted. "The stadium was filled with women and children. There's no way everybody would've made it out safe after I shot. People would've gotten hurt."

"Worrying about the lives of others wasn't your top priority," Anderson replied. "All that mattered to the government was putting an end to James Tyson's terrorism. Any loss incurred would've been considered collateral damage."

"Collateral damage?" Silver exclaimed. "These are kids we're talking about. They don't deserve that."

"No one deserves that, but we didn't have any choice in the matter," Anderson sighed. "It would have been for the greater good. Now, I know you grew up in foster care, and family is a touchy subject, but think of all the families Tyson has destroyed over the years. You blew one of the best chances we had at eliminating him. What're a few lives when compared to the loss of thousands?"

Silver sighed before sitting back down. "So, what are we going to do now?" he asked his friend.

"I have to report this failure to my superiors," Anderson replied. "We'll know what happens after I'm done meeting with them. In the meantime, go home and rest. I'll contact you sometime tomorrow."

"Alright then." Silver got up from the chair and shook hands with Anderson. "I'll see you tomorrow."

Instead of going straight home, Silver made a detour to his favorite bar in Downtown Manhattan. Worked up, he wanted a drink, and McLarens Pub was just the place for him. It was a small and cozy bar he discovered a couple of months after moving to New York. He had tailed one of his targets to the place one evening during a reconnaissance mission. He went for the job but stayed for the beer and warm atmosphere.

McLarens was one of the few bars in the city that had Silver's favorite drink. It was still early in the afternoon, so the place was empty when Silver arrived. Julia, his favorite bartender, was on duty, so he pulled up a stool and joined her. She was a red-bone and exotic looking. He remembered her telling him her mother was Irish-American and her father was Bahamian. That combination with a fit body and delightful smile made her alluring, and he felt his mystique attracted her to him. But neither acted on it—they were just very friendly with each other.

"Hey, Lee," she greeted him, whipping her long curly hair with a few thin braids at the temples over her shoulder. "You look like you've had a long day, and it's not even three yet."

"Hey, Jules," he said, nodding at her.

"Bad day at work?" she asked, wincing as she handed him a bottle.

Silver downed the whole thing before replying. "Something like that," he grunted. "Seems like it'll only get worse." He couldn't help but worry that he made a huge mistake letting Tyson go.

"That bad, huh?" Julia sympathized. "Is today the day you finally tell me what it is you do for a living? I know you work for the government only because I've seen your badge."

"Like I've told you every single time you asked," Silver smirked, "if I tell you what I do for a living, I'd have to kill you. And I'd miss you way too much if that happened."

"Ha-ha, very funny," Julia said, rolling her eyes. "Haven't you heard of bartender-customer privilege?"

"Nope," Silver replied. "I'm pretty sure that's not a real thing."

"You'd be surprised at how many drunk customers spill their guts to me," Julia said. "Like I was their shrink or something. And I've been told I give pretty great advice too."

"I'll be sure to take you up on your offer if I ever need a shrink," Silver said, smiling. "In the meantime, could I get another drink, please?"

"Sure thing." Julia sighed and said, "One of these days, I'll get you to spill your guts to me just like the rest do."

Silver watched as Julia went to fetch him another bottle from the fridge. For her sake, he hoped that day wouldn't come.

# CHAPTER TWO

THE BUZZING OF Silver's phone woke him. He unlocked it to discover the ping was a text Anderson sent him. His handler wanted them to meet near Upper Manhattan at 11:30 A.M., but the current time was 11:02 A.M. Silver jumped from the bed and threw on some clothes, nearly tripping over the bedsheets on his way out of the room.

It took him thirty minutes to reach the rendezvous point, which was a small café tucked in a corner of Harlem. When Silver walked in, he spotted Anderson occupying a small booth near the windows. The restaurant was virtually empty—save for two customers drinking coffee in a corner.

"You're late," Anderson said as soon as Silver sat across from him.

"I know," Silver replied. "Sorry. I got your message late."

"Rough night, huh?" Anderson asked. "Well, things are about to get rougher."

Silver frowned. "Let me guess, the higher-ups aren't happy I let Tyson go."

"You got that right," Anderson replied.

Silver sighed. "So, what's the verdict? Am I suspended or what?"

Anderson looked down at the table. "I'm sorry, Leroy," he said before placing his eyes back on Silver. "They want you to turn in your badge and weapons. Effective immediately, your contract has been terminated."

"Wait... what? They're firing me for this one incident? I've worked for them close to ten years now. I'm the best man in the whole unit! They can still use me, just not to kill a man in front of his daughter."

The waitress came to their table and poured them both a cup of coffee.

Anderson looked up and smiled at her.

Silver remained fixed on Anderson.

"I'll be back to take your orders," she said before walking away.

"Leroy, let's be reasonable here," Anderson said in a soft tone. "You ignored a direct order given to you when you let Tyson live. The higher-ups aren't too pleased about that. They hate it when people defy their orders. What did you think would happen?"

"I don't know, but I didn't think they'd terminate my contract so quickly. I'd assumed maybe they'd give me another shot to take Tyson out when he wasn't with his family. There were innocent lives at stake there."

"Well, we've missed a great opportunity with Tyson," Anderson said. "Yesterday's graduation ceremony was the best shot we had. Now, no one knows when he'll resurface again. It could take months or even years. And during that period, you can be assured that more lives will be threatened."

"Will I at least get my full pension?" Silver asked.

"That's the other problem here," Anderson said with a

sigh. "Due to the setback your lack of action caused, they tied up your money with lots of technicalities. You probably won't get anything out of it. And even if you do, it could take years."

"So, what you're saying is I'm jobless, and I won't get my pension?"

"I'm sorry, Leroy," Anderson apologized. "Honestly, I wish there was something I could do for you, but my hands are tied. I can't afford to ignore their orders. My family depends on me."

Silver was beyond disappointed. He didn't know what to do next. His skills and abilities were only suited for particular jobs, like the one he'd just gotten fired from. And without a college degree, his job prospects seemed pretty limited.

"I know you tried everything you could," Silver said to his friend. "It's not your fault I didn't follow through with my orders. It was nice working with you over the years."

Silver left the booth without touching his coffee. It was the farthest thing from his mind at the moment. His savings would only last him a couple of months before he went broke. Silver knew he had to start looking for a new job as soon as possible.

"Take care of yourself, Leroy," Anderson told him. "Don't do anything crazy, you hear me?"

"Thanks, man," Silver said with a smile. "I can't make any promises just yet."

"I'm serious," Anderson insisted. "Just lie low for a little while. I'll try to find a way to get your pension. I'm not making any promises, though."

"I know," Silver replied. "See you around." He walked out of the café and headed straight for his car with a clear destination in mind—McLarens.

Silver was occupying one of the corner booths when Julia walked into the bar later that evening. He wore a scowl and held a glass of amber-colored liquid in his hand.

"You alright, Leroy?" she asked, eyebrows drawing together.

"Yeah, I'm good," he responded, hardly looking up from his glass.

"You sure? Cause you don't look good," Julia said as she slid into the seat across from him. "How long have you been here?"

"I don't know," he shrugged. "Maybe sometime around noon? What does it matter? It's not like I have anywhere to be right now. I got fired today."

"Oh no, I'm sorry. But don't worry, we'll find you a new job in no time."

"And you know the worst part of it all?" Silver continued, ignoring Julia's attempt to be reasonable. "I don't even get my pension. After all the years I spent working for them. I was one of their best men!"

"Yeah, it sucks, I know," Julia said. "Why don't I call you a cab? I don't think you're in any condition to drive."

"I haven't finished my drink yet," Silver protested, not wanting to go home to his empty apartment yet.

"Okay, finish up," Julia directed. "But as soon as you're done, I'm calling the cab. Go sleep it off. Tomorrow we'll figure out what to do next."

Silver knew the chances of finding a job that required his particular skill set, a job he could truly stand behind, was pretty slim, but he just nodded as Julia headed over to the bar. Thirty minutes later, when he was ready to go home, true to her words, Julia got him a cab. He tried protesting that he was sober enough to drive himself, but she wasn't having any of his excuses.

The taxi dropped him in front of his apartment complex, and Silver made his way up the stairs to the place he'd called home for the past few years. The space was large enough to contain his few belongings—not that he had much of them in the first place. He'd always lived a minimalist life. Part of it was because of his line of work and having grown up in foster care. Silver tottered to his couch and plopped on it. He fished out the TV's remote from somewhere in the cracks of the cushions and hit the power button. He spent several minutes trying to find something to watch before settling on a basketball game. Maybe if he hadn't sustained the injury to his ACL, he'd have gotten a scholarship to play college ball. And who knows, perhaps his life would have turned out differently. After all, Silver had been a pretty decent basketball player in high school.

He sighed as he watched the players on the screen pass the ball to their teammates as if nothing else mattered in life but the game. He knew what it felt like playing as if your life depended on it.

"Well, there's no use dwelling on what might have been or not," he muttered to himself.

His meager savings would only cover a month and a half of rent and a few groceries, but after that, he'd be flat broke. As he drifted into a restless sleep, Silver wondered if he'd made a huge mistake, not killing Tyson when he had the chance.

# CHAPTER THREE

THREE WEEKS PASSED since Silver lost his job. And since that time, he hadn't left the house. He'd been surviving on pizza and takeout. On one particular morning, someone pounding on his door woke him from his alcohol-induced sleep. He'd left the television on—the noise from it added to his throbbing head. It felt like someone had cracked his skull open with a sledgehammer but didn't deliver the finishing blow.

The light from the TV wasn't helping matters either. Silver located the remote and turned it off. The pounding on the door was then accompanied by someone calling his name. Silver recognized the voice.

"How does she know where I live?" he muttered as he made his way to the front door and threw it open.

Julia had her fist raised as if she was about to continue assaulting his door. When she saw Silver had opened the door, she blushed.

"Did I wake you?"

"As a matter of fact, you did," Silver replied. "How'd you get my address?"

"Well, I did call you a cab the other day," she said, pushing past Silver to make her way into his living room. "And I still remember the address you gave the cab driver. Finding your unit was a bit tricky, though. But I have my ways."

"I can see that," Silver said, shutting the door behind him. He turned to see Julia staring at his messy apartment in horror. "Forgive the mess. I wasn't expecting company."

"This place looks like it suffered from an earthquake," Julia laughed. "I had to see if you were still alive. It's been three weeks, and you haven't come to pick up your car from the bar's parking lot. I was worried you'd done something crazy." Her face turned serious.

"It's been three weeks already?" Silver feigned a surprised look. He cleared out the empty pizza boxes from the couch and sat on it. "Make yourself comfortable," he said, gesturing to the space.

"Nah, I'm good standing," Julia said. "Wouldn't be surprised if a cockroach crawled out of that couch."

"Suit yourself," Silver shrugged. "Not like that's the worst thing to come out of there." He smirked.

"Well, now that I know you're very much alive," Julia said, turning toward the door. "Go get your car from the parking lot. McLarens has been threatening to have it towed if you don't move it."

"He wouldn't dare," Silver said, yawning. "I'm one of his favorite customers."

"Don't say I didn't warn you, though," Julia said with a shrug. She paused at the door. "Take a shower, clean up your apartment, and then drop by the bar so we can figure out what's next for you."

"I don't know if I can make it today," Silver told her. "I've got plans."

"Of course, you do," she replied. "See you around, Lee."

After Julia left, Silver groaned because he knew his pity party was ending. He'd wasted three weeks doing nothing to improve his finances. It was time for him to stop wallowing and look for a replacement job. Lucky for him, Julia wanted to help him out. He couldn't say he had any other options waiting for him.

Determined to retake control of his life, Silver got up from his couch and cleaned his apartment. After he took out the trash, he showered and headed for McLarens.

When he walked in, Julia was attending to a couple of customers. She smiled at him and mouthed that she'd be with him in a few minutes.

Silver perched on a stool at the far end of the bar. It didn't take long before Julia made her way to his corner.

"So, do you want a drink before we get down to business?" she asked him.

"I probably shouldn't," Silver said. The thought of beer didn't comfort him as much as usual. "I think I need to give my liver a chance to recover from my binge-fest."

"I hear you," Julia nodded. "So, do you have a college degree?" she asked, pulling out her phone.

"No," Silver replied. "I joined the army after high school. Didn't have the money for college."

"Okay, it might be hard, but we'll find something you're good at," she reassured him.

"It might take a while to find a job for a black man in his mid-thirties with no college education," Silver remarked.

"Don't be a naysayer," Julia commented. "Okay, let's start with this. What special skills do you have?"

*Besides killing people?* Silver thought. "I'm good with my hands, I guess," he said aloud. *I also know Kali, Muay Thai, and Jujitsu.*

"Hmm... that doesn't really specify much," Julia noted. "I just found a bouncer position on Craigslist. Think you fit that description?"

"And what exactly is the description?" he asked.

"Well, it's for a new club that opened up not too far from here. They need someone who can act tough and check people's ID at the door, handle things when people get too rowdy, you know."

"Sounds like a doorman."

"Pretty much," Julia agreed. "But the pay isn't too shabby. And you get free drinks."

"Anything else?"

"Well, not at the moment, but why don't you check out this one first and see how it goes? I'll text you the address of the place. Maybe you could go there tomorrow?"

"Fine," Silver said, resigning himself, "I guess it's better than doing nothing."

"Good," Julia exclaimed. "But if you could add a little bit more enthusiasm to your voice during your interview, it'd be great."

"I can't make any promises," he shrugged. "I'll go check out the place in the morning, though. It's not like I have anything better to do."

---

When Silver returned home later that night, he called one of his buddies from the military. Jon Bennett had served in the same regiment as Silver. He'd heard from Anderson that Bennett joined the NYPD and was running an undercover team with the Narcotics division.

Bennett had given Silver his number when the two had

crossed paths last year. Bennett picked up after the second ring.

"Hey, Jon," Silver said, "it's been ages."

"Leroy?" Bennett replied. "To what do I owe this surprise call?"

"I was bored and decided to check up on you," Silver answered. "It's been a while since I've heard that high-pitched voice of yours." He laughed.

"Of course, and I can hear yours is still as grumpy as ever," Bennett scoffed. "Anderson told me what happened to you. I'm sorry, man."

"Well, It—It's cool."

"It's not cool that they tied up your pension, though. If there's anything I can help you with, just let me know."

"Yeah, that's part of why I called," Silver said. "I need another job. I've just about gone through all my savings."

"I don't know of any openings," Bennett told him, "But I'll keep an eye out. You know—you could always join the NYPD."

"Nah, I'm done working for the government. I'm looking to branch out into the private sector. Know of anything in that area?"

"I'm not sure," Bennett paused a beat. "But I have a couple of leads I could check out. If anything clicks, I'll let you know."

"Thanks, man," Silver told his friend.

"It's cool. I've got to go now. Take care of yourself, Lee."

"Yeah, you too, stay safe," Silver replied, ending the call.

The conversation went better than he expected. He knew Bennett would find something. But since he didn't know when, Silver checked out the bouncer gig. It wouldn't do much in furthering his career, but since he needed to pay his bills, it'd have to do.

It was Silver's first day as a bouncer for Club Retro. Since it was near McLarens, Julia walked over and talked with the owner on Silver's behalf. One amusing interview later, he had the job.

Club Retro's building design and layout mimicked that of the eighties. Silver thought it looked like the owner. She was a short, stout, and grumpy Chinese woman dressed in a green retro pantsuit with a white boa around her neck, and she insisted he take out the Ms. and just call her Wong.

Her taciturn demeanor made him believe she couldn't speak much English, although if there was one thing he learned from his previous job, it was to assume nothing about anybody.

"You're hired," she said in clear, unaccented English after she looked him up and down, walking a slow circle around him.

Silver felt she was looking down on him, although he was more than twice her height. He assumed it had something to do with the commanding presence she possessed. A lesser man would have felt intimidated.

"Don't you want to conduct an interview or... is there anything you'd like to know about me?" he asked, turning to face her.

"Ever been arrested?" Wong asked.

"No," he replied.

"As I said, you're hired. You can start Friday," she said, looking him up and down again before walking away.

Silver watched her with his eyebrows raised and his mouth gaped. He then jolted his head and made his way to the exit. As he stood outside the club, Silver was sure that job would be short-term; it would bore him. Bennett had better come through—and quick.

The job consisted of standing at the door, checking the IDs of people who looked too young and throwing out any troublemakers. So far, a few high school seniors tried to use fake IDs to get past him, but he wasn't having it. No one caused any trouble yet, but like Julia told him before her shift, the night was still young. She also told him that the job required him to have patience—something he was quickly running out of.

On his previous job, and while he was in the military in Afghanistan, there were times he needed to be patient. With the promise of action ahead, he always found the adrenaline running through him very calming.

"Yo!" Dani, the bartender yelled. "That's enough! Get out before I call security to haul your drunk butt out of here."

Silver smiled. That was his cue, and he was finally going to see some action. He ran inside to check out the situation. A white male, in his mid-forties, was sitting by the bar, puking his guts out. Silver was not prepared for that sight, and dry-heaved twice before he convinced himself that he would not empty the meager contents of his stomach right next to the man.

"Not what you expected?" Dani asked, grimacing.

Still somewhat unsure if he would vomit, Silver put a hand over his mouth and pulled the man up from the bar stool none too gently. He herded the drunk toward the exit while Dani called for someone to clean up the mess.

"I'm so sorry, I... I didn't mean to cause any trouble, I just..." the drunk man said, retching as if more vomit was coming.

Silver let him go and backed away. The last thing he

needed was puke on him. It would make his already sucky day worse.

"It's alright," came Silver's gruff reply. "Happens to the best of us."

"Really?" the man asked, looking up with a smile on his face.

"Yeah," Silver replied, as he hailed a cab and helped the man get into it.

Silver's first shift didn't go much better after that. He ruffled and tossed out a young college male who thought slapping his high school girlfriend was the way to look all grown up and yelled at the girl when she stood up to follow her boyfriend out. He yelled at a celebrity who came by with her posse of girls because they kept squealing like baby seals.

Wong yelled at him for that one.

He went to the McLarens after his shift ended to get a drink where he described his night to Julia.

"She won't fire you, Lee. Don't worry, you'll be just fine," Julia told him between bouts of laughter.

"I hope she does," Silver grunted in reply. "It's only been one day but feels like I've been working there for months."

"Oh well, we need to look for another job real soon, huh?" Julia asked before tilting her head and smiling, showing all her teeth.

His responding grave nod sobered her up quickly.

# CHAPTER FOUR

JULIA SAT ON a stool at the kitchen counter in Silver's apartment while he cooked. She had adjusted her work schedule, so they had similar shifts and visited his place every other day. At first, Silver insisted Julia shouldn't be walking home alone, then he invited her up to his apartment for breakfast, and she was hooked. After that, she would crash on his couch while he went out to whatever site he was working at for that day.

Silver had picked up a day job as a handyman at a construction company. It helped him purge the adrenaline he stored up at Club Retro. He couldn't punch the trouble making drunks, so he needed another way to let out steam. Manual labor seemed to help some.

"Where did you learn to cook so well?" Julia asked as she pushed her plate toward him for a second helping.

"Something I picked up while I was in foster care. One of the foster parents didn't care much about feeding us kids, so, as the oldest one, I had to step up." Silver told her as he piled more spaghetti Bolognese on her plate.

"I learned growing up that cooking calmed me, so I

spent every free moment doing it, even while I was in the army and between assignments at my old job." He hid a small smile as Julia moaned while eating another bite.

"It's so good!" she enthused.

That was why he kept inviting her back for meals. She was a delight to cook for every single time.

"I know what you can do!" Julia exclaimed as if she'd just uncovered the secret to life. "You could be a chef for one of those fancy restaurants, and I bet they'll pay pretty well too."

"Nah, I don't think so. I never went to those fancy cooking schools," Silver replied, brushing the suggestion aside.

A few weeks passed and Silver was a cook at a restaurant. He paused mid chopping to laugh at the circumstances. Julia found a restaurant that was hiring for a cook. It was near his apartment, which made it convenient for him. He could never understand how she always found those places. She was like a job magnet.

Silver's official title was Junior Chef because of that fancy cooking school he never attended. Despite his lack of credentials, he was positive he could cook better than the Head Chef. He didn't let it bother him, because the job paid more than both the bouncer and construction jobs combined.

At first, Silver tried juggling both jobs, but when he beat up one of Club Retro's customers for attempting to force himself on one of the barmaids, Wong fired him. The guy was a big spender at the club, and Wong didn't want to lose him.

What did he care? He had a much better job now, anyway. A buzzing noise yanked Silver out of his thoughts. He pulled his phone from his pocket and looked at the caller ID. It was Bennett. Silver placed his knife on the counter and walked toward the back door.

"Where are you going?" yelled the Head Chef in a forced accent. His name was Giovanni, and he insisted he was Italian, even though everyone knew he was lying.

Silver ignored him and stepped outside to take the call. "Bennett," he answered.

"Hey man, how's it going?" Bennett greeted. The reception was choppy.

"I'm good. Where are you? I can barely hear a thing."

"Middle of a job," was Bennett's abrupt reply. "So, I'm calling about that job you asked for a little while back."

"Any luck?" Silver asked with little expectation, although he hoped Bennett had good news.

"Well," Bennett started, "you wanted to go into the private sector, right? I think I've got just the thing for you—a contract to hire position with a private company that handles weapons contracts for the feds, the military, and the whole lot of 'em."

"I'm going to need more details," Silver replied, trying hard not to get his hopes up.

"You've heard of the billionaire, Kirby Cush, of Cush Industries?" Bennett asked.

"Yeah, I know who she is," Silver acknowledged. "Her father, Gavin Cush, started the company back in the eighties. Although, back then, they weren't handling weapons contracts for the government. It wasn't until his daughter took over from him that they decided to branch out to other profitable ventures."

"Okay, well, long story short for now. She needs protection and you happen to be the best man for the job. Especially, as you currently have no ties to the government. Look, this is delicate work, so I obviously cannot share details over the phone. We're going to have to meet," Bennett concluded, already seeming to dismiss him, probably because of whatever job he was on at the moment.

"Got it. The usual spot?" Silver inquired.

"Uh-huh, you know the drill," was the distracted reply from Bennett.

Silver disconnected, feeling more enthusiastic about chopping and dicing condiments for his boss. But Giovanni's piercing voice yanked him from his reverie and into the moment. Silver was still in his thoughts and didn't understand what prompted Giovanni's outburst.

"Crap," Silver snapped, as he realized he was holding an uncut onion in his other hand. "Alright, alright, I'll get back to it," he said to Giovanni, who was now past complaining and just ranting.

"I'm the head chef. I'm not supposed to do all the work by myself like peasant slave," he wailed in a horrible Italian accent. Silver found it insulting, even though he wasn't Italian. He'd have probably punched Giovanni in his big nose if he had been born Italian.

"Everything I do by myself. If I want do everything by myself, I not hire anybody!" Giovanni yelled.

It was torture hearing him murder the language, so Silver tuned him out. Not even Giovanni's tirade was enough to dampen his spirits at that moment. He was about to go back to doing what he loved the most.

Silver floated around on his personal cloud all day, so much so that when he went to McLarens later that evening to get a drink, he could tell Julia knew something was up.

"Hey, cool cat," she said as Silver walked up to the bar. "I'm guessing if I checked, all the canary would be gone," she continued with a cheesy smile. "What's up? You finally hooked up with a woman?"

"I'm not even going to try to figure out what that first part is all about," Silver said. "And no, I didn't hookup with anyone." His smile deflated at Julia's assumptions.

"Grumpypants," she muttered. "What else could be making you so excited?"

After she returned from sending some drinks, she continued, already distracted from her former line of thought.

"Oh! There's that woman in the sexy, red suit. She's quickly becoming a regular around here. She's got that 'work-wound' type look written all over her. She looks like she needs someone to untangle her muscles properly. You should totally buy her a drink. It'll most certainly get you places," Julia said, pouring drinks into three shot glasses simultaneously.

"No, thank you, I don't need to unwind anybody," Silver replied, turning to check out the woman, anyway.

She was a brunette with thin lips and small white teeth. Her cherry red jumpsuit was fitted and sleeveless. She looked Silver's way and smiled before squinting and turning away.

Silver couldn't help but think he'd met her somewhere.

"Hey Jules, how long has she been coming around here?" he asked. Silver didn't last a decade in his former line of work by ignoring his instincts.

"Why? Are you interested? Should I send a drink over?"

she asked, crawling toward him on her tippy toes and grinning wide.

"Whoa, there, simmer down." Silver backed up. "There'll be no sending drinks or hookups with anybody."

"Aww, why do you always have to be such a buzz kill?" Julia pouted.

"Find someone else for her if you think she needs unwinding so bad," Silver said.

"Nah, there's no fun in that," Julia grumbled, peeking at the woman.

The woman glanced back in their direction.

"You know what? On second thought, stay far away from her," Silver told Julia, pulling some bills from his wallet to cover his drink.

"I knew you liked her. You can't pretend with me now..." Julia said with a smirk.

Silver scoffed as he stood. "Hey, I got to go now. Be very careful. No talking to strangers. You know the drill."

"Yeah, yeah. I'll call Raj for a ride straight home immediately after my shift," Julia said. "Don't think I forgot you didn't tell me what had you all happy earlier. You're all cagey, which naturally has me curious."

"If I told you, I'd have to kill you," was his standard but trite reply.

Silver heard Julia squealing at him on his way to the door. He didn't know what she thought she knew, but he hoped she kept it to herself. He already worried that someone from his past might hurt her, just because she had reached out to help him.

Silver knew he should have been more careful, but those early days were a blur, and when he woke up, she was already important to him. Julia had become his best friend and someone he could count on.

He waited for a few minutes, and then took his time circling around the block just to satisfy his paranoia and assure himself that she was indeed safe.

He stepped onto the subway platform and looked around out of habit. First, from his previous job, and second, as someone who had made New York their home for almost a decade. He walked out of the station and to a newspaper stand near the station. The place was empty, save for the man behind the counter.

The next day Silver left the restaurant just after the lunch rush hour. He hurried to catch the next train to Central Park. He looked back as he hurried away, still amazed by how easily he got permission from Giovanni to end his shift early.

"So uh, hey," Silver had started, nervous for some reason. "I... uh have to meet with someone important. Do you think I can have the rest of my shift off? I'll do an extra hour tomorrow."

Giovanni was in a rare, good mood. He had always expressed that Silver's life would be a lot more fun if he started seeing someone, and he smiled before shooing Silver out the door. Silver didn't know what to think of his reaction, but he also didn't want to tempt the fates that worked out that one for him.

He stepped onto the subway platform and looked around out of habit. First, from his previous job, and second, as someone who had made New York their home for almost a decade. He walked out of the station and to a newspaper stand near the station. The place was empty, save for the man behind the counter.

"Hey, mister, excuse me. That man over there asked me to..." a random young boy seemingly appeared from nowhere, tugging at Silver's jacket.

Silver judged him to be around ten or twelve. The boy wore a multicolored bicycle helmet and a T-shirt with some sort of superhero on it.

In the middle of the kid's speech, the boy turned to look behind himself, as though he expected to see someone. When he didn't find who he was looking for, the boy shrugged and thrust a New York Times paper at Silver until he took it. Then, he walked away briskly, without looking back—like he wanted to forget the entire thing.

Silver was sure Bennett had paid the boy to deliver the paper. With a shake of his head, he opened the newspaper and noticed a sticky note inside. Of course, Bennett wanted to be dramatic. He was an undercover narcotics detective, after all.

*Park bench facing the lake, Central Park, 30 minutes*, the note read.

Silver sighed and started toward Central Park. *Is all this really necessary?* he thought. They could have just met outside the precinct—at a coffee shop or even at Silver's job, but Bennett wanted all the cloak and dagger. Silver didn't much blame him; he knew Jon had always wanted to work for the FBI or CIA. He couldn't figure out why he hadn't gotten a job with them yet. Maybe they could sense how much he wanted it and decided to hold out on him.

When he got to Central Park, he spotted Bennett right away. Of course, that was probably why Langley didn't want him; he'd make a terrible spy. Walking up to him, Silver pulled down the enormous paper he used to block his view and then took off the aviator glasses his friend was wearing.

"Leroy, what are you doing?" Bennett said, surprised at Silver's antics.

"No self-respecting spy would ever be reading a giant newspaper while wearing dark shades, dressed like that, in the middle of Central Park, in the middle of the afternoon." Silver laughed at how ridiculous his friend looked.

He removed the baseball cap and scarf Bennett had on and started walking toward the mall.

"You looked like you were about to be shipped to Madagascar," Silver joked.

"I was totally pulling it off. Nobody knew who I was!" Bennett protested.

"This is what happens when analysts decide they want to go out into the field. They endanger everyone, starting with themselves." The teasing turned into a gentle chastisement, and it had the exact effect Silver was going for since Jon looked slightly remorseful and embarrassed.

*You should feel embarrassed.* Silver chuckled at the thought.

"So, Kirby Cush," Silver started as the teasing died out. "You said you had more to tell me about this contract to hire position."

"Yeah," Jon replied, falling in step with Silver. "So, you know Miss Cush, billionaire mogul in the aviation and weapons tech industry. She was contracted to do some work for the federal government and to make upgrades for the military."

Silver held up his hand to pause the conversation while they found a more suitable spot for conversation. They walked to the food court and stayed in line to get food. Both settled on a soda and bagel and then sat at an empty table in a corner where they could watch everyone coming and going.

"Cush Industries, hmm... What has she gotten herself into this time?" Silver asked, picking up where they left off.

"Wait, you know her history?" Bennett asked.

"Who doesn't? She's often in the paper," Silver shrugged. "What? Or should I say, who has she wronged this time around?"

"The matter is somewhat delicate, but in short, Miss Cush is going to need a new security package."

Silver sighed, preparing to decline. He was desperate for work, sure, but didn't want to babysit a trust fund baby, who'd most likely be a brat the entire time.

"Leroy, I need you to listen carefully. She's in real trouble. I wouldn't call you if I thought any different."

Silver and Bennett had met in the military and were in the same unit for an entire tour. All the time Silver had known Jon Bennett, he'd never heard him sound so worried before. It was almost enough to make Silver think Bennett had a good reason for attempting to disguise himself earlier. Something was up.

"You have my full attention," Silver replied.

"In her new government contract, Kirby is upgrading some of Langley's birds at St. Andrews."

"Her company is working for the CIA?" Silver asked, concerned about the connection to his old employer if he took whatever gig Bennett was proposing. "I thought they only did business with the military and maybe sometimes the FBI?"

"Well, yes. In the past, Cush Industries worked only with the military and the FBI," Bennett replied. "But they started collaborating on a project recently with the CIA. Most of the work is classified, so I don't have all the details," he continued. "But I know Kirby is doing most of the designs herself, for some obvious security reasons. Also, there's probably no one else smart enough to do what she's doing."

"Wow, okay... but how do you know so much about CIA business?"

"I'm not supposed to talk about it, but I guess you'll find out soon enough," Bennett said. "All the NYPD knows officially is that Kirby Cush is a business contractor. But last week, one of the CIA's planes ended up in the Atlantic, and we got word that it might have been tampered with. All that remained their problem, and Uncle Sam had no qualms about keeping it to himself. But Kirby lives in the wonderful state of New York, and two nights ago, someone shot at her as she was exiting a club downtown. We put a tail on her, but she keeps slipping them like she doesn't know it's for her own good." Bennett sighed into his soda.

"So, you want me to protect her while you guys figure out what's going on?" Silver asked.

"Yes, with a small team," Bennett held up a hand. "Now I know you like working alone. But it's only three people, and you'll be her primary contact. And yes, protecting her will be your main job, but we also want you to figure out what she knows and why someone's targeting her. Kirby clamped down every time we started asking her questions."

Silver was still processing everything when something occurred to him. "Wait, aren't you supposed to be in Narcotics?" he asked. "How does all this connect with what you do? Or is Kirby Cush also involved with drugs?"

"No, she isn't. Not that I know of," Bennett stated. "I'm not really with Narcotics anymore. I was recently bumped to spearhead a special task force. It's like a collaborative effort between the CIA and NYPD. Very few people know about it." He reached into his pocket and removed a brown envelope before handing it to Silver. Inside were pictures, notes, and some forms. "So, you in or what?"

"Let's do this." Silver stretched out his hand, and they shook on the deal.

# CHAPTER FIVE

LATER THAT WEEK, Silver was at work and annoyed. Giovanni was on a rampage, and no one was safe from his wrath. Granted, he never was a great example of the ideal boss, but his crankiness that day was off the charts. For some reason, only known to him, he was mad at everyone and kept finding faults in everything they did.

"What you doing, eh?" Giovanni snapped at Skylar, a waitress.

She trembled, probably wishing she was anywhere but Giovanni's kitchen. Skylar was a sweet little thing who wouldn't hurt a fly.

"You not know I running a business here, eh?" Giovanni asked, folding his arms and tapping his foot.

Skylar was on the verge of bursting into tears. She had been going about her regular morning routine of cleaning the wine bottles and cups, a task she now tackled as if her life depended on it. The way Giovanni was acting, it probably did, or at the very least, her job was at stake. It appeared he was looking for a scapegoat.

"Leave the poor girl alone, Jeff," Silver called as he walked out of the freezer.

"What you call me, Jeff?" Giovanni asked with disdain, "To you, I'm Chef Giovanni, or you don't work here anymore, eh?"

"I might just take you up on that offer, Jeff," Silver replied, stretching out the syllables in Giovanni's name.

The silence in the kitchen was deafening. Everyone had stopped what they were doing and stared at Silver, Skylar, and Giovanni.

Silver shrugged. "Consider this my twenty-four-hour notice," he said.

"Everybody out!" Giovanni yelled.

At that, everyone scrambled for the door. The kitchen and wait staff cleared out in record time.

Silver followed the horde toward the door.

"Not you, Leroy," Giovanni called, stopping Silver dead in his tracks.

"Yo, man, you can't leave..." Giovanni pleaded in a more natural east coast tone, which prompted a burst of laughter from Silver.

"No hard feelings, Jeff, my man, but I got a better offer."

"It's Kathy's kitchen, huh? I pay you double," he bargained, the fake Italian accent creeping back.

"Drop the act, man. You're not fooling anybody. We all know you're from Jersey. And no, I'm not taking a job at Kathy's or any of your competition. I'm just doing my thing."

Silver picked up a stack of vegetables and began dicing. Even though he'd just quit, he still had meals to prepare. It was the least he could do for the restaurant's customers—not that Giovanni deserved it.

After leaving work that evening, Silver felt he was being followed. He was on his way to a cafe in Downtown Manhattan to use their Wi-Fi and run a search on Kirby Cush. He wanted to see if he could find her on his own and get a feel of what to expect when he met her. But after noticing two men following him, he detoured home first to get his pistol.

When Silver left his apartment, he saw the men again. He was now positive he was being followed. He should have expected it sooner and started preparing for it a long time ago for several reasons. First, he had done the government's dirty work for the last decade. Second, he knew secrets they didn't want getting out. And finally, he had decommissioned rogue agents for them, so he knew the drill. In his line of work, it was easy to make dangerous enemies quickly. Silver was very good at his job, so of course, he had racked up enemies. He used a café downtown to surf the web because he developed a nagging feeling that something was going to happen to Julia because of him. He wanted to be within easy reach if that happened.

Silver strolled around the block that housed McLarens. Once he stood in front of the bar again, he looked through the windows and saw something that stopped him in his tracks. The woman in the red suit from the other night was back. But instead of a jumpsuit, she wore red sports leggings and a black tank top under a red zip-up hoodie. She was at the bar having what appeared to be a friendly chat with Julia.

*I thought I told her to stay away from that woman.*

Silver turned and headed toward the door, irritated. As he rounded the corner into the alley, he heard footsteps speed up behind him. Silver listened without breaking his stride; after all, there were just two of them.

*This should be easy*, he thought with a smile as he slipped his hand into his holster to take the safety off his 9mm Beretta, which was already connected to a mini suppressor. His mind ran through drills, preparing for anything that could come at him. Silver only used guns as a last resort, and it had been months since he had seen any action. He very much planned to enjoy this.

Silver heard the first shot clap from behind him. It was a suppressed round. *Professional hitmen,* he thought as he ducked and took cover behind two large metal dumpsters. As fast as he could, Silver sprung on top of the closed dumpsters and ran a couple of steps before jumping. He heard two more bullets penetrate the first dumpster as he pulled out his gun mid-air, shooting one of the men and smashing the butt of his gun into the head of the other man, who was closer to him.

Both men were sprawled on the pavement. Silver searched for a pulse on the guy he shot but didn't find one. He then checked the time on his own watch and waited for the one he knocked unconscious to wake up, so he could get some information from him. He didn't have to wait long.

"Welcome back," he said to the man.

The man adjusted himself to a sitting position on the ground. His hand immediately went to the bruise on his head, but he said nothing, and only peered at Silver.

"Who are you?" Silver asked, aiming his gun at the man.

The guy continued to stare at him.

"Who do you work for?"

The man remained silent.

"If you don't talk, I might have to hurt you," Silver said.

The main squinted but said nothing.

Silver knew he wouldn't get anywhere with the man. He had seen his type before and that guy wasn't going to speak.

Not wanting to waste any more time, Silver struck the man in the back of the head again, giving him another nap.

---

Silver watched McLarens' door from the corner. He wanted to see the moment Lady Red, as he'd taken to calling her in his head, stepped out. A few minutes passed before she exited. She smiled and waved at Julia before leaving the bar.

The lady paused and looked around as if she was waiting for someone. Instead of taking a cab, she walked down the block. Silver caught up to her, and she immediately swung her right elbow at his stomach, settling any questions about her suspicion as a threat.

He trapped the erring elbow with one hand and twisted it toward her back, as if he was going to put cuffs on her. Silver followed up with a swat to the back of her neck.

She ducked, dampening the effects of the blow.

"I was told to expect better!" Lady Red replied as she dealt a savage kick to his shin, freeing herself and following it up with another to his head.

Silver grunted and staggered backward.

She regained her footing and ran into the alley.

"Why are you following me?" Silver asked as he raced after her, looking to his left, then his right before fixing his sights on her.

She was clearly a professional, so whoever had sent her was not messing around. Instead of answering him, she fired off a flurry of kicks, each of which he blocked. He grabbed her right foot and yanked it, but she braced against the wall and aimed at his head with her other foot.

Silver blocked that kick too and gave her a push to the chest.

She spun in the air and dropped to the ground, breaking her fall with her hands and then sprang back to her feet. She exhaled then threw a quick jab at Silver.

He deflected her punch with his hand and retaliated with a kick to her gut and then to her head in quick succession. She barely dodged both blows.

"Who do you work for?" Silver continued, charging the attack with a roundhouse kick to the still staggering woman. "Talk!" he growled, giving her space to reorient herself.

"We'll get to that when I'm done here," she responded, darting toward Silver.

"Then let's get done here, shall we?" Silver replied, determined to end the fight.

They exchanged several punches and kicks. Both landed a few on the other. She kneed his groin, and he doubled over. She followed with a savage elbow to his spine, but Silver kicked her legs from under her. The impact sent her straight onto the pavement, headfirst. He followed her to the ground and held her in a chokehold until she passed out. He lifted her, bridal style, and walked back along the alley into the street and hailed a cab.

"What are you doing?" Julia asked from behind him.

"Jules, I'm going to need you to step back inside, right now, please," Silver demanded, standing still, hoping she'd listen for once.

"Oh my, are you finally hooking up with a woman?" Julia asked with an enormous grin before frowning. "Wait, is that blood?" she stammered as she ran in front of him. Julia's eyes widened when she saw how disheveled Silver looked in the faint light.

"What did you do to her?" she exclaimed, looking at the unconscious woman.

"Jules, please keep your voice down!" He admonished in

a loud whisper. "Also, go back inside, call Raj, and get out of here now!"

When she didn't budge, Silver knew he had to change his commanding tone to a more pleading one so she'd understand the gravity of the situation.

"Please, Jules, I need you to trust me right now. I promise I'll explain as much as I can later," he implored.

Julia finally snapped to action, realizing where they were and how much trouble the circumstances could spell for Silver. "I'm coming with you. And you're going to explain everything," she muttered as she reached for her phone to order a Lyft.

---

Silver paced the length of the guest room in his apartment, trying to collect his thoughts and plan his next move. Julia sat in the corner, gazing across the room with her mouth open. Silver told her he was a government assassin and was sure she was still processing it. He kept it short and was vague with the details of his work, only telling her enough so she understood the seriousness of their situation and why he needed her to leave town for a few weeks.

Lady Red was tied up and lying on the bed. She'd wake soon, and he needed Julia gone by the time she did. He didn't want to further involve her. If the woman saw Julia with him, it would put her in more danger.

Finally, with a curt nod and strong eye contact, Julia stood. "Fine, my parents have been asking me to visit for months now; this might be a good time to catch up on family time," she said.

Silver smiled in appreciation. "Thanks, Jules," he said, as

he reached to hug her. "This whole thing will be over soon, and you can have your life back," he promised.

With a kiss to his cheek, she whispered, "You'll be careful, right?"

Silver nodded, and she stepped out of the apartment. He turned to find piercing blue eyes, watching him with amusement.

"Aww, how touching. Is she your girlfriend? Wait, then why was she trying to set us up?" came a sarcastic voice from the bed.

Silver went to the chair he had placed in front of her. She struggled to sit up in the enormous bed.

"Ah, ah." Silver pointed his 9mm at her face. "I ask the questions here. You answer truthfully, or I blow off your pretty little face and get my answers elsewhere," he said in an eerily calm voice.

"No need to threaten me," the woman said in a monotone voice. "I've been awake for the last thirty minutes. I heard you narrate your sorry story to the pretty bartender. It was both sweet and sad."

"Get to the point," Silver growled.

"I won't tell you my name, for both our sakes." She shrugged. "But I was sent to kill you."

"Okay, why?" he waved his gun as he spoke.

"Sorry, but you're a loose end," she said. "You didn't complete an assignment. And that's a no-no," she concluded, shaking her head and tsking.

Silver sighed. "Right, so, the government that burned me sent a self-righteous mouthpiece to neutralize me, instead of pursuing the real bad guy."

The room went silent for a moment.

"Did Anderson send you?" Silver blurted, standing still as he waited for her reply.

"No," she said softly, as if she could understand that this was not the time for anything more than a direct answer. "The command came from way above his pay grade. More than likely, he's not even aware of the hit placed on you."

Silver released a breath he didn't realize he inhaled. It would have been ten times worse if Anderson, who he considered a friend, had ordered his death.

"Look, I don't want to kill you," Silver started. "So, if you're willing, I have a message for the ones who sent you. And a small favor to ask," he concluded, removing her bonds and checking her head for injuries.

"What's your message?" she asked, eyebrows raised.

"I'm back to working for the government, so I'd like to set up a meeting with the higher-ups, so they know to leave me alone," he stated.

Lady Red pursed her lips. "I don't know if that would be entirely possible. I'll see what I can do, though."

"In the meantime, if you could also not send any more of your goons to kill me, you know, just until all this is over. I would really appreciate it," he added. "It'd be quite stressful watching my back while trying to do my job."

"What goons?" the woman asked.

"The guys you sent ahead of you, so you wouldn't have to get your hands dirty," Silver told her.

"What are you talking about?" Lady Red asked, the perplexing frown on her face getting deeper with each accusation.

Silver squinted. "Two men tried to kill me earlier today," he said. "I thought they were with you since you showed up right after them."

"Well, did you ask them nicely, the same way you've asked me?"

"They weren't talking," Silver replied. "And they had nothing on them that provided clues of who sent them."

"Well, that's too bad for you," she shrugged. "I suppose you've racked up a list of enemies a mile long. News that the government is no longer protecting you must be spreading, and they're coming to collect. I heard James Tyson found out about the attempt on his life and fled. Even he would want a piece of you," she said with a sarcastic snort. "Your life is going to be so much fun now. I'm so jealous."

Silver didn't know if she was joking. He couldn't tell from the poker face she wore. "Yeah, whatever. I don't find more trouble fun."

"Well, is that it?" the lady inquired. "That's all you want?"

"No, not exactly," Silver said, trying to put his thoughts in order. The news of the possible bounty on his head made him lose his train of thought.

"Well? Are you going to tell me what this favor is or not? Because I'd really like to get out of this dump."

Silver snapped out of his inner musings and handed her a business card.

"That's Anderson," he told her. "Tell him I need to collect the favor he owes me. He'll understand what I mean."

# CHAPTER SIX

AFTER A MONTH of relative inactivity, Silver's life went from boring to action-packed, and he wouldn't have it any other way. His problems were still unresolved but were the kind of issues he had trained for.

He took a cab to Kirby Cush's home on the Upper East Side. She had called that morning and told him to report to her house and even offered to send a town car for him, but he had declined the ride. The house was a mansion sitting on a massive estate. Silver didn't even bother trying to guess the value of the property. An enormous gate blocked the public from seeing inside the property.

The cab driver rang the bell at the gate and waited. The intercom scratched, followed by a female sighing.

"Come on in," she said.

A moment later, the gate buzzed open, and they drove through. A butler waited for Silver near the entrance. He ushered him inside and Silver stood alone in the foyer for five minutes. Soon after, a young maid exited a room near the staircase and slowly gaited to him.

"I'm sorry, Mr. Silver, but you'll have to wait a little

longer," she said in a flat voice. "Ms. Cush is quite busy at the moment," she finished, her gaze wandering.

Silver gave a quick nod.

"Follow me. I'll show you to her study."

Silver followed the young lady upstairs and through a set of double doors. The room was spacious, and large pictures covered the walls. A colorful antique rug dressed the floor, the bookshelves stood tall, and at the far end of the room sat a desk with an executive chair behind it. On the wall, behind the chair, was a security panel.

"Wait here. Ms. Cush will be with you shortly," the girl said before leaving the room.

Silver spent several more minutes in the room admiring the portraits. When he ran out of pictures of cranky, old, white men to look at, he began inspecting the security panel behind her desk when Kirby entered.

"Sorry to keep you waiting for so long," a husky voice said, pulling him out of his reverie.

Silver turned to see Kirby Cush enter the study with another woman trailing her. Kirby was a tall blonde, about six feet, and in her late twenties. She looked like she did in the dossier pictures.

"Impressed?" she asked with a proud smile, nodding at the security panel he'd been studying.

She wore workout clothes and appeared to have just finished a rigorous session. Silver figured the other woman was a personal trainer because she was also wearing workout clothes.

"I'll see you Monday, Kirby," the trainer said, giving Kirby a fist bump and tossing a brief nod at Silver in acknowledgment of his presence.

He nodded in return and watched her leave the room.

"I'm Kirby Cush," Kirby said, introducing herself with a

smile as the doors closed behind the trainer. "But you already know that, don't you?"

Silver nodded in response. "Yes, ma'am."

She wrinkled her nose at the 'ma'am' remark but said nothing otherwise.

"I'm Leroy Silver, pleased to meet you," he said, extending his hand to grasp hers in a firm but brief handshake.

"Solid, that was quite a grip," Kirby said after the handshake.

Silver's face remained expressionless. "I thought this was going to be a meeting for the whole team. Where is everybody else?" he inquired, looking over her shoulder and at the double doors.

"I was curious about you. I hear you're the best. Tell me about yourself, work experience and all."

When Silver raised his eyebrow at the request, Kirby quickly continued.

"I... I need to know I'm safe... and can trust you," she said.

"Well, my name is Leroy Silver, as I already mentioned," he started. "I served in the army for eight years. Two tours in Afghanistan." He paused, noticing the slight nod Kirby gave as he spoke. It was as if he was confirming something she already knew. "Proficient in firearms, hand-to-hand combat, tactical awareness, and a general tough guy," Silver quipped. "None of which you don't already know, I guess, seeing as you have read my portfolio."

Kirby raised her eyebrows at his last statement. "I just have one question," she said.

"Sure."

"In your portfolio, there's a ten-year gap between when you left the army and now. So, tell me, what went on then? If you don't mind my asking, of course." Kirby paused. "I mean, you don't just leave the army, with no record of your activities, and then pop up as the best choice for a security package."

"I don't mind, but that's classified information, ma'am. I'm sorry," Silver said, his expression showing no remorse. "I'm going to need you to walk me through the happenings surrounding your life and business these past few months," he said, redirecting the conversation.

Kirby pursed her lips and looked at the floor.

"I can't do a proper job of protecting you if I don't know what your activities have been and what your routines are," Silver explained. "My job is only fifty percent dependent on my skill sets. The other half, Ms. Cush, depends on your transparency. I can't protect you from things I don't know about."

"Alright then, where do we start?" Kirby asked, getting right to business.

"Maybe the shooting you were involved in, or your connection to the CIA's plane in the middle of the Atlantic," Silver suggested taking a seat at the edge of Kirby's work desk.

"Right," Kirby said, sitting on the sofa opposite him, "Just one thing before we get started, Mr. Silver?"

"Yes?" he asked.

"Call me, Kirby," she said.

---

"I'm Sergeant Derrick Landon," a tall, familiar-looking, blond-haired man said, standing at the head of the conference room in the NYPD District 12 Precinct. Pointing at himself, he continued with, "Weapons expert."

"That is Sergeant Luke Walker," he indicated to an unassuming man, with mousy brown hair, glasses, and a forgettable face. "Undercover agent."

Silver figured it made sense for him to be an undercover agent since he had one of those faces. The kind that wouldn't stand out in a sea of faces.

"Semy will join us in a minute. She works tech magic," Landon continued, leaning forward as if he was getting ready to share a secret. "Tell her that, and you might have made a friend for life... or not. Semy is well, Semy... You'll see what I'm talking about soon."

A petite Asian woman walked in. She was somewhere between her early to mid-thirties. She walked straight to the projector, inserted a data pen, and then stood at the front.

Landon came to sit beside Silver. "Don't ask Semy if her height and name are related in any way," Landon whispered in Silver's ear. "She hates it when people do that. Trust me when I say you don't want to upset her."

"Got it," Silver replied, with an acknowledging nod. He had met many tech types, and they always had peculiarities. He knew this Semy chick wouldn't be any different.

"Semy," she said, pointing at herself with both hands, while she did a little curtsey. "I have the blueprint of the aircraft upgrades made by Kirby Cush and her team for the CIA. And, I have superimposed it with the original template," Semy started, diving right in and starting the meeting. No one bothered to introduce Silver and Bennett; that was cool with Silver. "The CIA already ran algorithms to compare both, and they came up with a few discrepancies," Semy continued. "Someone, either on the CIA's team or Kirby's sabotaged it. And they're working on providing us with anything they think will be helpful to us."

"Of course, they get to be the judge of what is deemed helpful or not," Sergeant Walker muttered.

Silver smiled. *Ah, the age-old fight between law enforcement and the bigwigs.* He just hoped they didn't drag him into it. He had his own issues to handle.

Semy shot Walker a glare and continued her presentation. "They discovered a blueprint that matches the final engineering, and all the other planes are exactly as expected," she said, changing the slides to show another blueprint. "Indicating that it wasn't an engineering error. Someone wanted that specific plane to go down." She grumbled the next part. "Of course, they don't feel it would help us if we knew why they targeted that specific plane. But we figure it was probably the same reason why someone tried to kill Kirby. We have to figure out what happened and prevent any more attacks."

"Shouldn't the Feds be handling this?" Silver interjected. "Or even the CIA?"

"Leroy Silver, is it?" Semy peered briefly into a dossier on the table, sharing her gaze between it and Silver.

"Yeah, that's me," Silver replied.

"Well, Mr. Silver," Semy continued. "While it is the job of the Feds to handle things like this, we've been hired by Ms. Cush because she doesn't want to place all her eggs in one basket. I'm not saying the CIA or FBI won't do a good job, but we both know there tend to be unnecessary bureaucracies involved with these situations."

"So, we're basically doing their job for them," Silver noted.

"If that's how you want to see it," Semy replied. "The primary aim is to protect Ms. Cush. We can only do that by finding out who poses a threat to her. More than likely, they're the same people who sunk the aircraft, so I guess we're investigating that too. Hence the collaboration with the CIA."

"Interesting," Silver grunted.

With no further questions, Semy finished up her presentation and left the projection running for the next person who'd present. The rest of the briefing continued with the five of them brainstorming their next line of action. They concluded the CIA would handle most of the work. There wasn't much they could do about that. Their top priority was figuring out who attacked Kirby and why.

CHAPTER SEVEN

THE FIRST TWO weeks on the new job were quiet. Still, Silver knew better than to let his guard down. He spent the time getting to know his new team. Kirby offered them all lodging in her mansion to make their job easier, and all took her up on the offer, except Derrick Landon. He cited personal reasons for not committing to staying at the house. Silver didn't make a big deal out of it because Landon always made it on time to any important team meeting.

They trained every day, and it became apparent that Kirby wasn't just doing sexy body workouts or Pilates with her trainer. She kept up with all the drills and simulations Silver conducted for them.

Semy and Kirby worked tirelessly on examining her plane designs for what could have attracted the assassination attempt. They exchanged ideas, bickered, and became close friends. From time to time, Silver left them to check up on things at his house. He also did a little digging to find out more about the person who had sent those two goons to kill him. Since no one had come for him again, he assumed Lady Red had delivered his message to Anderson.

"You know the drill," Silver started. "Always stay within arm's reach, and if you ever need to take a detour from the original routine, let me know so we can initiate an emergency strategy immediately. We can't—"

"—create any window for the enemy to hit us," Kirby said, finishing his speech. "I know the drill. Also, it'll be fine. Nothing is going to happen, same as the past two weeks," Kirby said, straying from Silver and toward the window to stare outside. She stood there to expose herself as a target to prove that she wasn't a sniper's mark. "See, I'm not dead," she said, walking from the window and through the door to the foyer. "Shall we?" She paused at the door, a smile on her face as she held out her hand to Semy, who was closest to her. "We don't want to be late now, do we?"

Kirby was going to meet with the shareholders for one of her companies. And from there, she'd head over to Cush Industries for another meeting. Silver and the others were accompanying her as they'd done over the past few weeks whenever she had to leave the house.

"Of course not. After you, my lady," Semy demurred with a perfectly executed bow and sweep.

Kirby pseudo swooned, and they all laughed. Silver felt they were just silly.

Suddenly, there was a loud snap, followed by Kirby falling face-first onto the front porch. The thud of Kirby's body smacking the ground brought all Silver's worse case scenarios to the fore. Everyone was where they needed to be. She'd walked out behind Landon, who was supposed to have swept the area ahead, and before Semy, who watched her back. Everything was in place, and everyone in position.

*So, what happened?* Silver wondered.

Thoughts of horror flashed across his mind in rapid succession. "*Why did she fall? Was she dead? How could this happen just one step past the door? Why did he let her walk ahead of him? Why did he let his guard down with the self-pacifying excuse of still being within her premises? Just why?"*

"Kirby!" Semy yelled, kneeling beside her.

Landon raced across the yard, his head swiveling around the property.

Silver stepped around Semy and went to Kirby's other side, turning her gently. A painful groan tore from her throat and Silver exhaled.

"You're alive, thank God." He examined her, and his fears began dissipating.

"Hey, I'm fine," she replied, brushing him off. "My heel snapped, that's all. Although I wish something less mortifying had happened," she muttered with a forced smile.

They took Kirby's executive car. A shiny black limousine with chrome trimming that sat eight. For Silver, the best feature of the car is that it was bulletproof.

The trip to the first meeting and then Cush industries was uneventful. Kirby breaking a shoe heel was the only exciting thing to happen that morning.

They all cleared out of Kirby's office as she connected with Langley to make a call to the CIA. They insisted Silver and his team couldn't be privy to the call as a matter of national security. Silver argued that he needed to be present to do his job, but no one paid him any mind.

Kirby had asked for a slight detour on their way home after the meetings. And after that morning's episode, Silver was feeling a little sorry for her, so he obliged. She had directed Walker to a cemetery, and she walked to a polished gravestone with fresh flowers. No one had asked her who the grave belonged to; neither did she volunteer the information. Kirby dropped a small toy by the grave and stood to leave after five minutes. There were tears in her eyes, which she quickly wiped away as she returned. No one said anything as they made their way back to the car.

Everyone piled into the limo and headed for home. Halfway through the trip, Sliver noticed Walker peering in the rearview mirror. Silver looked back and saw an SUV tailing them at fifteen yards. Shrugging it off, he faced the front and looked into the review mirror. Walker was staring back at him with wide eyes. Silver glanced behind but jerked off balance as the SUV rammed them on the passenger side.

Silver nudged Kirby down between the seats.

Walker swerved, avoiding a second hit.

Landon looked out the window and yelled, "Silver! Your end." As Landon was speaking, another SUV rammed into them from the driver's side. Silver rolled down the window, pulled out his gun, and fired at the car closest to him while Landon began shooting at the other vehicle.

Walker sped up, inching away from the two pursuing vehicles. Two men from one SUV and a blonde-haired woman from the other shot at the limo.

While Silver shot at their assailants, Landon fished out a grenade from his bag. He popped open the sunroof and stood halfway out, yelling for Silver to cover him.

The grenade pin dropped to the floorboard. A few seconds later, Landon crouched inside the limo, and there was a thunderous blast. The SUV on the driver's side caught fire and somersaulted twice before sliding into the guardrail. The other SUV stopped chasing them and turned back toward the blazing vehicle.

Silver felt tempted to turn around and give chase, but he had Kirby—whose life he couldn't endanger—on the floor, quietly sobbing into her hands. Semy was drawing circles on her back to calm her down. It appeared to work some because the intensity of Kirby's sobs eased. Silver, not wanting to expose Kirby to further danger, ordered Walker to drive them straight home.

***

Silver had not been to his house for the last few days. He'd spent most of his time with Semy at the NYPD, reviewing security tapes for any clues to who their attackers were. The lack of information was disturbing. He stopped by his place to pick up a few clothes and other essentials. Even though Kirby had been a gracious host, it somehow felt awkward. Plus, he wanted to check on his apartment. While there he took a nap and when he woke, there was a missed call and voice message on his phone.

He pushed the button to play the voice mail and heard Anderson's voice.

"Hey man, sorry I haven't kept in touch, things have been crazy... even crazier than when you left. I got your message. We can meet using our old drop point system. I'll be there first thing tomorrow morning."

Silver mentally rearranged his schedule to accommodate the meeting with Anderson. He knew Landon and Walker could hold down the fort in his absence, and Kirby would be in great hands until he returned.

***

The next morning Silver was on his way to the drop point when he saw Anderson waiting outside the subway station.

"What are you doing here? This isn't where we are supposed to meet," Silver said with his head on a swivel.

He flinched as Anderson hugged him but relaxed after a beat and returned the hug.

"Aww, you missed me," Anderson teased as he released Silver with one final pat on the back.

"Not necessarily," Silver grunted. "Just didn't want to leave you hanging there."

"I promise, I didn't know about the hit placed on you," Anderson stated after they'd separated. "If I'd known about it, I'd have tried to stop it or given you a heads up."

"I know," Silver said with a slight smile. "I figured you couldn't live in a world without me."

Anderson smiled and nodded. "Were you followed?" he asked.

Silver titled his head and scoffed. "You're the one who's been behind a desk all these years. I should be asking you that."

"Fair enough," Anderson chuckled. "Let's go."

They headed to a coffee shop a couple of blocks away from the subway station so they could talk privately.

Silver told Anderson about everything he'd been dealing with.

"Sounds like you've got your hands full with protecting Ms. Cush," Anderson stated after Silver finished talking.

"Yeah, it sure seems that way," Silver replied, taking a sip from his coffee. It was too hot, so he pushed it aside to let it cool down. "Anyway, now to the reason I sent the message." Silver turned to look Anderson in the eye. "I need you to convince the higher-ups that it's not in their best interest to keep sending people after me."

"Yeah, that's already been handled," Anderson said. "Langley already hit the brakes on your case after you took the contract with Kirby Cush. I guess by the time they got the news about your employment, the hit order was already sent to the female operative who came after you. They couldn't stop that one in time."

"How convenient for them," Silver said, shaking his head. "So, if I wasn't so observant, I'd probably be dead right now."

Anderson shrugged. "You obviously didn't last this long without being attentive to your surroundings."

"Now, about the other goons who attacked me that night," Silver continued. "Got any idea if Tyson found out I was sent to kill him?"

"That's highly unlikely," Anderson said, holding his chin while wrinkles crossed his forehead. "That's unless he has people on the inside, which I wouldn't put past him. If he does, it means the whole operation has been compromised."

"Either way, I need you to help me figure out who sent those guys," Silver said.

"It'd be hard," Anderson told him, "But I'll try my best to get something tangible for you soon."

"Thanks, man," Silver said, taking a sip from his now cooler coffee.

"Don't thank me yet, until I find something."

They talked for another hour before they both got up and left in opposite directions.

As Silver headed back to Kirby's estate, he began replaying the most recent attempt on Kirby's life. Somewhere in the back of his mind, he kept wondering if it was the people trying to kill Kirby who attacked them or the ones after him. Whoever they were, it still didn't explain how they knew exactly where they would be. It all pointed to a mole somewhere in the operation.

Silver was also worried about Julia. There was still no word from her since she left for her parents' place upstate. He, however, took no news as good news.

Silver tossed and turned the entire night and only fell into a fitful sleep in the early hours of the next day.

At the team meeting that day, everyone was cranky as though they all had a horrible night like him. Semy was the only one that looked normal, but Silver didn't know if it was because she was okay or because she always had a calm, detached demeanor.

"I got a hit, people," she announced as she flopped to the middle of Kirby's den with a computer tablet in hand. The team had set up shop there and turned the place into their makeshift command center. "I pulled the SUV's plates from traffic cam images in the area and ran it through a... a unique tracking software. It's on the move, this time somewhere near..." she paused, looking at the tablet before continuing. "The Cush Industries' warehouse in Queens. What could possibly be in your warehouse?" she asked, looking at Kirby.

"That's our assembling warehouse, so it mostly has parts..." Kirby broke off, looking up as if a thought had struck her. "The CIA stalled my production plans after the incident with the last plane. Before that, I was designing a commercial plane with a state-of-the-art stealth system."

"Sounds like a brilliant idea," Walker said, winking at her.

"Why would you build something like that?" Semy asked with genuine curiosity. "What commercial plane would need a stealth mode? Oh... right," she trailed off as everyone's eyes landed on her.

"It's not meant to be a commercial plane," Kirby stated. "It was meant for covert operations."

"So, why'd the CIA halt your productions?" Silver asked.

"I'm not entirely sure," Kirby responded. "But they did

say they wanted to investigate what happened with the last aircraft that crashed."

"It's great that we're trying to figure out what's going on and all," Landon interjected. "But can we start heading to the warehouse to see what's going on there before it's too late?"

---

They piled into two cars. Landon drove one—with Semy as his only passenger, and Walker drove the other with Silver and Kirby. Silver was reluctant to bring Kirby in proximity of possible shooters. But she reminded him that she was the only one who would know if something was missing and what it was. Kirby also emphasized that, as he always said, she was safer with them more than if she stayed at home alone.

The trip to the warehouse was quiet, but no one relaxed or dropped their guard. It was as though they all knew this was just the calm before the storm.

"Landon, do a quick sweep of the area; the rest of us will get to the warehouse to check things out," Silver said.

Semy got out of Landon's vehicle and hopped into the back seat of the other.

Landon headed out to scan the perimeter while the rest of the team proceeded to the building.

"Semy, any updates?" Silver asked from his position in front.

"No, the car still looks like it's parked in the warehouse parking lot," She replied, looking up from her tablet. "It feels like we're walking into a trap."

"I know. Could we plan a decoy?" Silver stopped scanning the area and turned to face them.

When they all nodded, he continued talking.

"Semy, I want you to come into the building with me," he continued. "Walker, stay with Kirby, but you must be ready to drive away at a moment's notice. I have a feeling this could go south fast, so we must be alert and ready to move."

Kirby had been briefing them about the contents of the warehouse on their drive over to the place. She said the most important thing was the blueprint for the model she'd designed. They would grab it and take it back to the NYPD. Silver felt it would be safer there than at Langley. At least the NYPD wasn't compromised yet. Or so they hoped.

"How come you didn't just keep the model in your house?" Walker asked, his eyes still on the road.

"Well, at the time, I didn't think anything would happen to it at the warehouse," Kirby stated. "Besides, I have an encrypted copy somewhere on my computer. And the designers needed it to do their work."

"Landon, what's the news?" Silver asked over the comms.

"All quiet, sir," Landon said in a casual tone.

"Alright, let me know the moment that changes," Silver instructed.

"You got it, chief," Landon replied, and the comms went silent.

"You guys ready?" Silver asked, addressing Walker, Semy, and Kirby in the car.

"All good, Silver," Walker responded.

"The rich one is scared pale," Semy reported from the backseat.

Kirby swatted at her.

"Hey!"

"Children, quiet down please," Silver teased.

Kirby had called ahead to let the security in the building know that she was coming and wouldn't be alone. At the checkpoint, Walker lowered the backseat window, so the guards could see that she was in the car.

"Hey Billy, Devin," Kirby greeted each of them with a friendly nod.

"Good afternoon, Ms. Cush," the older of the two replied as he opened the barrier and let them through.

"Smart, and polite to the help," Semy said to Kirby with a smile. "There's hope for you yet."

Kirby snorted in response.

When they arrived at the parking lot, there were no other cars there, except for the delivery vehicles they sometimes used. No one in the group said anything about it. They resolved to get the blueprint out of the building and transport it somewhere safer.

Semy and Silver headed to Kirby's office in the warehouse. They found the blueprint and headed out.

"Well, that was easy," Semy commented as they walked toward their car.

"Don't jinx it," Silver said with so much seriousness that Semy looked at him in surprise. "Landon, any update?" he asked, placing a finger to his ear. "Landon?" he repeated when there wasn't a reply. "Walker?" Silver called out, sounding panicked as he hurried, almost dragging Semy along behind him.

"Uh oh," Semy whispered. "I think I jinxed us," she said, pointing across the parking lot to the security checkpoint where Billy and Devin sprawled across the ground in pools of their blood.

"Walker, go!" Silver barked into his comm. The car engine revved, and the tires screeched as Walker followed Silver's orders.

Silver and Semy broke into a sprint, trying to get to the car before it was too late.

The sound of glass cracking, a woman's shrieking, and more tire squealing pierced the air. Two dark SUVs raced toward Kirby's vehicle. They shot at the car, and the window on the right side splintered.

Thankfully, that wasn't the side where Kirby was sitting.

"Where in the world is Landon!" Silver growled as he pulled out his 9mm and returned fire. They were closing up on the vehicles. Semy pulled her Glock and joined him.

"Leroy, look out!" she yelled, already diving over some barrels.

Silver followed her as he heard a grenade pin pulled, then saw that grenade tossed their way. An explosion roared and he prayed the drums didn't contain a flammable liquid. In a matter of microseconds, the flare from the explosion died down and Silver fired a few rounds at the fuel tank of the SUV shooting at Kirby's vehicle. After a couple of shots, he hit the target, and the SUV erupted into flames.

Walker turned their car and faced the other SUV. He shot the driver in the chest, and Semy got the one riding shotgun. With the driver dead, the SUV kept moving until it crashed into one of the parked delivery vans. Walker stopped the car in front of Silver and Semy and got out of the vehicle. Silver left them to take out the remaining two shooters while he checked on Kirby, who had ducked behind the backseat door.

The gunfire ceased, and Silver assessed the damage to their car. The windows were fractured. The car was covered with chips and scrapes from bullets, and the front dented. Another car's engine revived, and everyone pointed their guns in that direction until they realized it was just Landon.

The car looked a little worse for wear—it was cratered on either side, but at least, it could still move.

After Silver made sure everyone was okay, they drove straight to the NYPD to meet up with Bennett. Everyone was quiet the entire ride, ruminating and trying to make sense of what had happened.

"Hey, are you okay?" Semy asked Kirby.

Silver was proud of Kirby. Their training had paid off. She'd kept her cool throughout the entire gunfight and she wasn't as shaken up as she was after the first encounter at the cemetery.

"Yeah, I'm fine, thank you very much, you guys," she said to the team. Landon grunted in reply. Semy and Walker smiled at her.

"We're just doing the job you're undoubtedly paying us a lot of money to do," Silver said.

They laughed. The mood improved, and everyone was more open for the rest of the ride.

They safely delivered the blueprint to Bennett. Silver told him to keep it to himself for the time being. And after giving her statement about the incident at her warehouse, Kirby made a big announcement.

# CHAPTER EIGHT

"YOU WANT TO take a vacation?" Walker asked when they were back at Kirby's estate.

"Yeah," Kirby replied. She fished out a bottle of Chardonnay from her wine fridge and poured herself a glass. She indicated where the wine glasses were for anyone interested in joining her and plopped on the couch in the den.

"Care to tell us why you want to leave your already secured house and go elsewhere?" Landon asked.

Semy, having gotten some more wine glasses from the kitchen, poured wine for herself and settled next to Kirby.

Silver watched the two women from across the room. He was standing near the window, checking out the surroundings, waiting for Kirby's reply.

"Well, I just realized that the plan may not have been to just kill me," Kirby continued. "But rather intimidate me for the blueprints."

"And what's to say they won't still continue targeting you even after you leave?" Silver asked.

"The NYPD has the blueprint," she stated. "If my suspicions about a mole are true, they'll tell—whomever, that the blueprint was given to Bennett."

"Hmm…" Silver grunted. "I think you leaving might be a good idea."

They turned to look at Silver.

"You do?" Kirby asked. "I assumed you hate the idea."

"How secure is this Swiss villa?" he asked, a thought forming in his head. During their drive back to the estate, Silver had arrived at the same conclusions Kirby had expressed earlier. It would make sense why there wasn't a more direct assassination attempt at her. A sniper or explosive expert could have gotten the job done quickly with little manpower. It was definitely possible they wanted her alive. Getting her out of town for a while might be a good idea.

"The villa is quite secure, I assure you," Kirby stated. "It has a private security team, and only a handful of people know the exact location."

"If it's as secure as you claim," Landon said, "how come you didn't head there after they came after you the first time?"

"Because if she'd gone, she wouldn't have found out what they were after," Silver told Landon.

"What he said," Kirby replied, nodding. "Plus, I had some businesses to attend to before going underground, so to speak."

---

Later that night, after Landon left for the day and the others retired to their rooms, Silver and Kirby remained in the den.

"So, what happens after you leave?" Silver asked. He'd been wondering if Kirby would end his contract since it appeared she didn't need his services anymore.

"What do you mean?" Kirby asked, looking up from her laptop, which she'd typed on furiously for the last thirty minutes.

"Should I start looking for a new job now that you're leaving for your well-guarded vacation villa?"

"No, you still have a job to do," Kirby said. "The fact that I'm going underground doesn't mean there's no longer a threat to my project and Cush Industries. Someone is trying to destroy everything I've built, and I don't intend on letting that happen."

"Okay."

"You came highly recommended," Kirby continued. "And I've learned to trust your instincts. I'd like you to remain on the grounds to look after things and figure out what's going on and who's behind everything. Think of this as a permanent position—even after everything is resolved."

"Sounds like a plan," Silver nodded. "I think it'd be a good idea for you to take someone from the team, either Semy or Walker. That way, it'd be easier for me to get in touch with you and make sure you're safe."

"I need Semy here with you," Kirby said, "She'll make your job a lot easier. I'll take Luke with me. He's great at keeping a low profile."

"Agreed."

A couple of days had passed since Kirby Cush left for her private villa somewhere in the Swiss mountains. She'd told Silver and his team to stay in her mansion since it afforded them easy access to her encrypted network, which ensured private communications. Silver also convinced her to limit the housekeepers' and groundskeepers' access to the mansion while she was away.

Everything had been calm since then. Semy tried to retrieve more from the dead guys' files, to figure out who hired them. She'd been searching their transactions and calls but found nothing worth mentioning.

Silver had heard nothing from Anderson since their last meeting. He didn't know if that was a good sign or a bad one. And no word from Julia either.

At that thought, Silver's phone rang with the caller ID showing an unknown number. When he picked up the call and heard Julia's voice, he let out a breath he didn't know he was holding.

"Hey, Lee," she greeted, excitement in her voice.

"Hey, Jules," he replied. "Good to see you're still your same cheerful self and remember how to use a phone."

"Don't get smart with me," she laughed. "The network here is spotty. I had to go into town to get decent cell reception. I don't know how my folks manage to live this far from civilization."

"I guess it helps that they're not millennials," he told her. "They're used to it."

"Well, at least the Wi-Fi here isn't as bad as the cell reception," Julia acknowledged. "I don't think I'd survive if I was completely cut off from the world."

"All that matters is that you're safe," Silver said. "I was beginning to worry when I didn't hear from you."

"I'm good," Julia replied. "The only thing here that could kill me is boredom. But hey, at least I've got Internet TV."

"Of course, you do," Silver laughed.

"I've got to go now. My phone's about to run out of juice —forgot to charge it last night."

"It's cool. I'm just glad you're okay."

"Yeah, same here," Julia replied. "Take care of yourself, Lee. Don't do anything stupid while I'm gone."

"I can't promise I won't," he said before ending the call.

Later that night, Silver got an email from Anderson with potential leads. He checked the time; it was close to midnight.

"He should still be awake," Silver muttered to himself.

Anderson picked up on the third ring.

"Don't tell me you're already asleep?" Silver said in the way of a greeting.

"Well, some of us have day jobs," Anderson grunted. "Couldn't you have waited until morning to call?"

"It's already morning," Silver replied, watching as the clock on his nightstand hit midnight.

"You know what I mean," Anderson sighed. "I'm guessing you got my email?"

"Yeah, I didn't get a chance to check it earlier."

"Okay. Well, anyways, I tried looking into the two guys who attacked you," Anderson continued. "We didn't find much on them until we looked into their accounts. A day before they showed up looking for you, someone wired payments into their bank accounts. I can't do much with that information without tipping off the wrong people. I figured with your new resources, you'd be better suited for the task."

"Yeah, I'm pretty sure Semy can trace the payments and find out where they originated from."

"Good. Now, can I go back to sleep? I've got to be up in a few hours."

"Sure, go get your beauty sleep," Silver teased. "Thanks again for bailing me out," he said in a serious tone.

"Yeah, any time," Anderson replied and hung up.

Silver forwarded the mail he'd received from Anderson

to Semy. He figured she'd be asleep and wouldn't see the message until the morning. A few minutes after he'd shut his eyes to sleep, his phone started buzzing. The caller ID showed it was Semy calling.

"Hey, you got my message?" he said, answering the phone.

"Meet me in the den," was all she said before ending the call.

Silver threw on a shirt and headed for the den. Semy was typing away on her laptop when he got there. A cup of coffee steamed next to her elbow.

She looked up as Silver entered. "I found a connection between the accounts you sent me and the one belonging to the guys we took out at the warehouse," she said.

"Seriously, that fast?"

Semy gave him a look that asked if he doubted her skills.

"Don't underestimate the power of a cool decryption software and my investigative mind," she told him. "Besides, I was already working on this before I got your email. It didn't take me long to find a connection."

"So, what's the connection?" Silver asked, taking a seat next to Semy and peering into her laptop. All he saw was a bunch of numbers jumbled together. He couldn't make heads or tails of it.

"First off, who owns those accounts you sent me?" Semy asked.

"They belonged to the two goons who tried to kill me a while back," he said. "I asked my friend—former superior, Anderson, to check into them for me. The only thing he could find were these accounts."

"These accounts might help us with our case," Semy stated.

"Care to shed more light on it?"

"Give me a couple of minutes, and I'll provide a solid lead for us to check out pretty soon," she said, turning back to her computer and typing. "I just have to decrypt some code to uncover who the last two accounts belong to," she muttered. "It's like a spider web of codes here."

"Okay," Silver nodded, "You do your thing while I sit here and watch cluelessly."

Several minutes passed before Semy exclaimed, "Eureka! I've found it!"

"Good, now it's time to share with the class."

"Okay, okay, don't get your undies in a twist," Semy teased. "Wait, shouldn't Landon be here for this?" she asked.

"There's no time," Silver grunted. "I'll brief him in the morning. This is exactly why he should be staying in the mansion with us."

"Alright," Semy said. "So, back to what I was saying. It turns out the people who tried to kill you work for the same person who attacked Kirby."

Silver sighed. "Right, but how did you figure that out?" he asked.

"The money."

"What about it?"

"A wise person once said, 'When in doubt, always follow the money.' It always leads you to the culprit."

"Sounds like a line straight out of a movie."

"Our perps all received money from an offshore account, sometime last month. At first, I couldn't trace where the payments originated because of some high-end encryption. It's probably why your friend didn't get much from the accounts. Decrypting the code required a high-tech program, which very few people use. Luckily, I'm one of them."

"Thank God for that," Silver said with a smile.

"I still haven't figured out who owns the account that paid your assassins and Kirby's assailants," Semy said. "However, I traced another account that received a payment a few weeks ago. It belongs to a David Kim from Long Island. I was able to use his Social Security number to find his current address. According to his LinkedIn account, David works for Cush Industries. He's one of their designers."

"Wow, so we've got our mole?" Silver asked. "Does he have any priors?"

"None that I can see," she replied. "He seems like a decent guy—probably just got greedy and decided to sell information to make a quick buck."

"If that's the case, he's in way over his head, and we have to get to him before someone else does."

"Yeah, you're right. Kim seems like a loose end, one that might be tied up sooner rather than later."

"I'll send a message for Landon to get here first thing in the morning and brief him on everything we've uncovered. We'll head out immediately to find Kim and bring him back here for questioning," Silver said, getting up from his seat. "I need to shut my eyes for a few hours. You should get some sleep too. We wouldn't want you to overwork that precious brain of yours."

"I'll turn in shortly," Semy replied, "I just have to check out a few more leads. I'm still uncovering more payments sent from the same offshore account. It's as if they're not even trying very hard to hide these transactions. It's crazy."

"Okay, I'll see you later," Silver told her before heading back to his room.

Silver woke to noise coming from the kitchen. On his way to check on it, he smelled freshly brewed coffee and found Landon sitting at the kitchen counter, watching the news on the huge, flat-screen TV.

"Good morning," he greeted Silver upon sighting.

"Good morning," Silver replied. "You got my message, right?" he asked.

"Yup," Landon said, taking a sip from his coffee mug. "I made coffee and got breakfast," he continued, pointing to a box of doughnuts and bagels on the counter. "It's the least I could do for missing out on the fun last night," he said, shrugging.

"Thanks, man," Silver said, reaching for a mug and pouring coffee into it.

After helping himself to a reasonable number of dough-nuts and bagels, Silver briefed Landon on everything Semy uncovered the previous night.

"Wow," Landon exclaimed. "Sounds like we've got our first, big lead on this case."

"Yeah, it's about time we started figuring out what's going on," Silver stated. "Have you seen Semy this morning?"

"Nah, I think she's still sleeping. The den was empty when I got here."

"I'll go check up on her. We should head for David Kim's place soon."

Landon said nothing, just nodded.

After Silver finished up his breakfast, he went looking for Semy. When he got to her room, which was on the same floor as his, he stretched out his hands to knock.

"Semy, we're about to head out to David Kim's place," he said through the closed door. "You plan on joining us?" he asked.

There wasn't any reply from inside, so Silver pounded on the door again.

"Semy?" he called.

"What's with all the racket?" he heard her ask from behind him.

Silver turned to see her coming out of the bathroom a couple of feet away from him.

"Sorry," he grinned. "I thought you were inside, sleeping."

"I've been awake since the crack of dawn," she informed him. "Just decided to take a bathroom break."

"Did you sleep at all?" Silver asked, worried Semy wouldn't be on top of her game if she didn't get enough rest.

"Yeah, I did," she replied, walking past him to her room. It was the same as his, except tidier. Her bed was made with the comforter draped equally on both sides. The floor, the dresser top, and the desk were free of any loose articles of clothing or paper.

Silver just stood at the doorway and watched as Semy got behind her desk and typed on her computer.

"I'm guessing you don't plan on joining us?" he asked.

"You're right," came her reply. "I've still got work to do. And I'm this close to discovering who owns that account," she said, lifting her hand and spreading her thumb and index finger an inch apart.

"Alright then. I'll leave you to work your tech magic while Landon and I check out Kim's apartment."

"Okay, keep me posted."

"Will do," he replied, closing her door and heading back to the kitchen.

Near the kitchen, he heard Landon whispering into the phone. He wasn't able to catch any of the words since Landon ended the call as soon as he approached.

"Was just informing my wife that I might be working late tonight and not to wait up," he explained. "She tends to worry a lot when I don't check in with her."

"It's cool," Silver told him. "I didn't know you were married, though."

"Yeah, we don't talk about our personal lives, that's why. We ready to move?"

"Yes," Silver replied, checking the cartridges of his gun to see if he had enough ammo. Not satisfied with what he found, he slid open a cabinet door, grabbed extra magazines, and stashed them inside his holster.

"Is Semy not joining us?" Landon asked, looking around as if expecting Semy to show up at any moment.

"No, she's not," Silver replied. "Semy is still working on a couple of leads. She said we should go without her."

"Okay," Landon got up from his chair and moved toward the front exit. "Let's get this road trip started. How long does it take to get to Long Island again?" he asked as they made their way to the garage.

They took one of Kirby's SUVs.

"About an hour plus," Silver replied, opening the SUV door and sitting behind the wheel.

Landon entered on the front passenger side. "Well," he replied, buckling his seatbelt. "Let's get moving."

---

Thirty minutes into the journey, Landon cleared his throat. He'd been glancing at his phone ever since they left the mansion.

"You're quite the man of mystery, Leroy Silver," he commented. "There's not a lot in your file after your time in the military."

"For good reasons," Silver grunted. "You researched me?"

"Well, I wanted to find out as much I could about the man I was entrusting my life to," Landon shrugged.

"Hmm…" Silver grunted.

"So, you married?" Landon continued, "Got a special someone in your life?"

"Nope," Silver answered, "I've found it's not a good idea to get attached in our line of work."

"That sounds depressing. I agree it's not always easy, but we've all got to settle down sometime."

"How come you never mentioned you were married before today?"

"I—I guess it never came up," Landon replied in a low tone. "We've all been too focused on protecting Kirby to talk about anything else."

At that moment, Silver realized he should have done his research on Landon and the other members of the team before joining. He'd assumed since Bennett hand-picked them, they could be trusted. After all, Jon was his friend, and he trusted him with his life. Even so, anyone could make mistakes.

Landon went silent for a minute, appearing lost in thought.

"Hey, how'd Bennett contact you for this job?" Silver asked.

Landon's forehead wrinkled at the sudden change in topic. "I was recommended to Bennett by my superiors," he said. "I guess something about my being one of the best weapons experts they had."

"So, you don't actually know Bennett personally?"

"Nope, I don't think any of us knew him before-hand," Landon replied. "Except for you, that is," he added. "Why do you ask?" Landon asked, eyebrows raised.

"No particular reason. Just trying to get to know you guys better."

"Yeah... right."

Silver slowed the car and made a right turn onto a side street. They snaked up the road for a minute before reaching a parking lot.

"Looks like we're here," he announced.

David Kim lived in a low-rise apartment building with a magnificent view of the park behind them. The grounds were clean and quiet, with little street or foot traffic.

"It's showtime," Landon said, removing his seatbelt and getting out of the car.

"This is a simple recovery mission," Silver told him. "We go in, get Kim, and get out. No violence required."

"And what happens if Kim refuses to come quietly?"

"I guess we'll just have to let Mr. Kim know it's in his best interest to come with us," Silver shrugged.

They walked into the apartment building and found the elevator had an *Out-of-order* sign in front of it, so they headed for the stairs.

David Kim lived on the third floor, so the climb wasn't awful; not that Silver minded. He'd faced worse. He recalled one assignment in Asia where he had to run up twelve flights of stairs to escape the police after strangling a homicidal dictator.

When they arrived at David Kim's door, Silver stood on one side of it, while Landon covered the other end.

"Mr. Kim," Silver called as he knocked on the door. "We're with the NYPD, and we'd like to have a word with you."

Landon raised an eyebrow at the white lie, but Silver shrugged. It didn't matter what title they used.

There wasn't any reply, and no sounds came from the apartment. Silver tried knocking again before trying the door handle. It was open. He gestured for Landon to cover him as he made his way into the room, gun cocked and ready. Silver scanned the apartment for any signs of Kim before he found him sprawled in the bathtub with a hole in his forehead.

"Looks like we were late to the party. Someone got to Kim before us," he said as Landon entered the bathroom.

"That sucks," Landon sighed. "Now we're back to square one—without any leads."

"Hmm… it would seem that way."

"I'll go inform Semy about Kim, so she can report it," Landon said, leaving Silver in the dead guy's apartment.

*Something didn't add up. Why was Kim inside his bathtub fully dressed? Did the killer instruct him to enter the tub, or was he moved afterward?*

A quick scan of the apartment led Silver to believe that professionals had scrubbed the place. He was pretty sure that if a forensics team showed up, they wouldn't find any prints apart from the victim's.

A boarding pass on David Kim's kitchen counter revealed that he was planning on leaving the States. He'd booked a one-way ticket to Paris. Unfortunately, he wasn't fast enough. Silver knew Kim was a loose end, but it appeared he was killed just before they arrived, which led Sliver to believe whoever ordered Kim's death knew they were coming to find him.

Silver and Landon left Kim's house to return to the mansion, and halfway through the trip, Silver received a text from Semy.

*I found something interesting. Let me know when you're close to the mansion. I want to take a nap before you get here.*

Silver hoped it was something huge to make up for the setback they'd just experienced. He wanted to wait until they got Kim before updating Kirby about their progress, hoping to share good news with her. But with Kim's death, their leads went dry.

Landon was napping in the passenger seat with his phone in his lap. The screen lit up with a message from someone named Summer. He opened his eyes and quickly placed the phone in his pocket.

*Who's Summer?* Silver wondered. *His wife?*

# CHAPTER NINE

WHEN THEY ENTERED the city, Silver stopped at a gas station near the house to fill up the tank. While the meter was running, Landon went into the store to buy some snacks.

Silver used the opportunity to call Semy. He walked a few feet away from the SUV before placing the call.

"Hey," Semy said, picking up on the second ring. "I'm guessing you're almost here?"

"Yeah," Silver said. "Made a pit stop to buy gas and snacks for Landon."

"Alright then."

"Semy, did you send the same text you sent to me to Landon's phone?"

"No, I sent it to you and figured you'd tell him. Why? Something happened between you two?"

"Nothing, we'll talk when I get back," Silver said, hanging up the call amidst Semy's protest when he heard the gas pump click.

Landon made his way back to the car, and they continued their journey to Kirby's estate. When they got back, Landon waited until after they briefed Kirby during their weekly video calls before stating he had a family emergency to handle.

Shortly after he left, Semy turned to face Silver.

"I know you told me not to say anything until Landon left," she said. "What's up?"

"That's what I need your help figuring out. Something's up with Landon, I'm not sure what."

"You're suspecting he might be the mole, right?"

"Something like that. Could you work your tech magic and see what you can dig up on him? Maybe pull his files and anything important."

"Hmm... and what happens if he's clean?" Semy asked, opening her laptop.

"Well, even if I'm wrong, he'd be none the wiser," Silver said. "It's why I didn't mention anything to Kirby about my suspicions. I don't want to go about accusing people based on my gut feeling—even though they've never failed me before."

A few minutes passed before Semy spoke.

"I was able to pull some of Landon's files," she said. "But most of it has been redacted. The clear part seems to contain the basic stuff, like health records, next of kin, emergency contact, etc."

"And isn't there any way to figure out what's under the redacted sections?" Silver asked.

"I don't think so. If it was the regular redacting method used here, I'd have been able to reverse it. But this right here is military-grade. The words underneath have been deleted and can't be recovered except with the original documents."

"A simple no would've sufficed," Silver muttered.

Semy laughed, "That wouldn't have been enough for you."

"Maybe," he said. Something occurred to Silver just then. "Hey, check if he's got a family member named Summer," he said.

"As a matter of fact, he does," Semy replied. "Summer Perkins. She's Landon's sister."

"How come they have different last names? She's married?"

"Yeah, but she got divorced a few years ago. Summer probably decided to keep the last name instead of going back to her maiden name."

"Initially, I thought Summer was his wife's name," Silver muttered. "Landon kept bringing up his wife during the trip."

"I dunno," Semy said, shrugging. "Maybe he was trying to set you on the wrong path?"

"So, there's no record of him ever being married?"

"Hold on. I just found something. It turns out Landon was married—briefly, a couple of years back, but his wife died shortly after their wedding from complications during childbirth."

"That's sad," Silver remarked, "but it still doesn't add up." He began pacing the den, trying to figure out how Derrick Landon was involved in it all.

"Maybe this might help," Semy announced.

Silver made his way back to her computer.

"It turns out Landon's sister, Summer, used to work as Gavin Cush's assistant," she said. "Reports show that there might have been an affair between the two of them."

"Things just keep getting more interesting," Silver mused. "Gavin was married at the time, right?" he asked.

"Yeah, they both were. Things went south between the two, and Gavin tried to cover it up by paying Summer off. And when Summer refused to let things go, Gavin's people threatened her. Somehow, she got into an accident—something about a faulty engine or such."

"You can bet Landon believed there was foul play."

"She didn't die from the crash," Semy continued, peering at her laptop screen. "But she wasn't the same either. This report I'm reading says she had some kind of brain injury and was placed in a group home by her husband, who later remarried. And with Summer's infidelity, I'm sure it was easy for him to get a judge willing to end their marriage regardless of her inability to sign the divorce papers."

"Sounds like a lot of family drama," Silver said. "I can see why Landon might hate Gavin Cush and everyone connected to him. But why not just go after Gavin directly?"

"I don't know," Semy shrugged. "Maybe he's not powerful enough to reach him directly. But add a hefty payment from someone who wants to take down Cush Industries into the mix, and Landon's motives increases. Oh... I just uncovered the name of the owner of the last account. It belongs to Ricky Summers, who I'm guessing is actually Derrick Landon."

"Nice work, genius," Silver smiled at Semy.

"And guess who's been paying the money to all these accounts," she continued.

"Who?" Silver was curious.

"Lincoln Power Plant."

"Never heard of it."

"That's because it's a shell corporation owned by the war criminal, James Tyson," Semy said.

Silver took in a breath, followed by a quick exhale. "If I'd just done my job and taken out Tyson like I was ordered several months ago," he grumbled, shaking his head. "None of this would've happened."

"None of what?"

"It doesn't matter. Before we take any definitive actions or contact Kirby, is there any other way to link Landon with James Tyson?"

"Is a picture of the two when they were cadets in the same military regiment proof enough for you?" Semy asked, turning her screen for Silver to see.

"This should be good enough for now," he replied. "How did you find it?"

"You can find anything on the Internet; you just have to know where to look," she said with a smirk.

"It's a good thing I never doubted your skills," Silver said, smiling. "We have to give Kirby a call and let her know what we've found."

---

"Since we stopped Tyson from stealing the blueprints. He may try to storm the warehouse and take the actual prototype," Kirby said through speaker phone, after they briefed her on the situation.

"I'm guessing by now, he already knows how large the plane is," she continued, "They'll come prepared. He'll most likely have his men disassemble the parts and take them out of my warehouse—bit by bit."

"There's strict security in the warehouse, right?" Silver asked her.

"Yes," she replied. "After the last incident, I doubled the security detail, but it still won't be enough to handle Tyson's men. I might have to reach out to the CIA and NYPD for help. Although, the problem of whom to trust among them remains."

"I can vouch for Bennett. I don't know if Anderson would want to get involved, though."

"Alright, round up who you can and head for the warehouse as soon as possible," Kirby said. "Semy, get to the command center and change the passwords. That way, Landon won't have physical access to the prototypes."

"Can't I do it from here?" Semy asked. "I mean, it'd be faster than waiting until we get to the warehouse."

"Unfortunately, you can't," Kirby sighed. "The servers are encrypted, which means you'll have to get inside and tap into the network before any changes can be made."

"Let's get to it," Silver said. "Landon already has a few hours head start. Hopefully, he doesn't know we're on to him."

"But are we sure Tyson would try to take the prototype by force?" Semy asked. "Cush Industries isn't just some small company he can bully into submission."

"Tyson isn't above playing dirty to get what he wants," Kirby said. "He wouldn't let anyone stand in his way, even if it means killing me or anyone in my family. He's bought himself immunity in several countries where he can hide out until everything settles down. He can send his goons to do his bidding from any part of the world he's hiding in without having to move an inch."

"We'll keep you posted," Silver said before ending the call. "Let's head out," he told Semy.

"We'll need more firepower than we have now," she said, sliding her laptop and a couple of Beretta M9s into a small backpack.

"I've got that part covered. Kirby gave me the passcode for the armory. Between what we have now and what's there, I think we should be covered."

"Sounds like a plan, just don't forget the code," she said with a playful smile.

"I have an excellent memory," Silver said, smiling back. "But if it slips, Kirby told me to get this from her office," he continued, lifting a small key from his pocket.

"What is it?"

Silver shrugged. "She said it's for a panel that bypasses the vault's locking mechanism."

"Good to know," Semy replied as they left the mansion.

During the drive to the warehouse, Silver contacted Bennett, informed him of the situation, and told him to meet up with them at their destination. He then tried calling Anderson but didn't get an answer.

In less than thirty minutes, they arrived at the warehouse compound. The security at the gate let them in without any questions. Silver figured Kirby had already called ahead to inform the guards of the situation. They were wearing bulletproof vests underneath their uniforms and had their weapons ready by their side.

"Any uninvited guests show up yet?" Silver asked one of them.

"No," the man replied, "It's been quiet since Ms. Cush called. We've searched the building's perimeter twice. The place is clear."

"Okay, that's good," Silver said. "Keep an eye out in case anything changes."

After they parked the car in the garage, Bennett and five other men pulled up in a black SUV.

He met Silver and Semy at the entrance of the building. "Thought you guys had started the party without me," he said as he approached with two duffle bags in hand.

Semy looked at the bags, squinted eyes.

Bennett shared his gaze between her and the bags. "We

came with our own weapons," he said. "It probably won't be enough if Tyson sends an army of men to attack the place."

"Sure. We've got more inside," Semy said. "I'm going to find the control room," she said to Silver.

"Copy that," he replied as she left them and headed inside the building. "Bennett, you and your men can cover the vantage points of the warehouse. The weapons vault is on the second floor. I'm going there now to see what we can use from Kirby's collection. If Landon or Tyson's men show up, let us know through the comms."

"Sure thing," Bennett said. "We've got this covered. Go get the weapons."

Silver patted his friend on the back and entered the building. He jogged across the empty, dimly lit lobby toward the elevators. He pressed the up arrow and the elevator door dinged open, emitting a beam of light into the lobby.

Shortly after, the elevator doors thumped closed, and the carriage jerked into motion. As the elevator slid upward, there was a roaring blast. The carriage shook and the lights snapped dark.

"Great," Silver muttered to himself. "The one time I decide not to take the stairs."

## CHAPTER TEN

SILVER HEARD GUNFIRE and explosions coming from outside the building.

"Bennett, what's going on?" he yelled into the comms. "Bennett? Semy? Guys, can you hear me?"

It didn't take him long to realize the comms were dead, and so was his cellphone. The only thing that could have killed the comms, phone lines, and the power to the building was an EMP. Silver didn't put it past Tyson to have one with him. The war criminal probably was crazy enough to use an Electromagnetic Pulse device to take down an entire block if he wanted something badly enough.

*And if so, it would mean the cameras are dead, and we don't have eyes on the building. It would also mean Landon knew we found out about him, and they've come prepared to fight.*

Silver needed to get out of the elevator A.S.A.P. He noticed a hatch on the ceiling and climbed onto the metal grab bar at the back of the carriage and stood, balancing himself as he pulled the latch. It clanked, and he pushed against the hatch, but it only budged. He adjusted his footing on the thin beam, palmed the wall for support, and gave it a hard shove. It thrust open and crashed against the metallic alloy of the elevator's roof. Silver jumped through the narrow hatchway and heaved himself up into the shaft before standing on top of the car. Level two was right above him. He used the guide rails to climb up, and when he made it to the second floor, he cracked the door open with his hands. The hall was empty, so he continued prying the doors apart before crawling into the darkened hallway.

According to Kirby, the vault was on the far end of the corridor. On his way there, Silver stopped at one of the vast windows overlooking the front entrance and saw a few bodies on the ground. Among them were the security guards who had been on duty.

The second window on the opposite side overlooked the parking garage. Silver looked out of it and saw a large Mack truck idling near the entrance with two men wearing masks standing beside it. They both held automatic rifles and were talking into satellite phones.

James Tyson stepped out of an SUV parked a few yards from the truck and made his way into the building.

Silver had no idea how many men there were or what parts of the building they were in, but he knew they hadn't made it to the second floor yet. He quickly made his way to the vault, the code in his head now pretty much useless due to the EMP. He searched the vault's door. Sliding his hand inside the jamb and patting near the keypad, he felt a small budge under the panel. The tiny compartment was incon-spicuous, invisible to the naked eye. Silver knelt and saw a keyhole underneath it.

"There you are," he uttered, digging into his pocket and removing the key he retrieved from Kirby's home office.

When he turned the key, a latch clicked. He pressed the small compartment door, and it swung open, exposing a lever. Silver pulled the lever and turned it clockwise. The sound of bolts thumping and scraping followed, and the vault door slid open. Light shone from the vault. Silver looked up and saw LED bulbs on the ceiling, battery-powered, he figured. Inside, the temperature was cool, and a clean metallic smell filled the air. A long bench covered with knives, handguns, and ammunition was at the center of the room. Larger guns hung on the side walls, and a tall cabinet was at the back. Sliver snatched two Sig MPX submachine guns from the wall, some extra magazines from the bench, and stuffed them into his duffle bag. Knowing he would possibly need to fight from a distance, he settled an SRS-A2 compact sniper rifle into the bag as well. For close-quarters combat, he grabbed two retractable nightsticks from the bench and tossed them into the bag. Inside the cabinet were several satellite phones. Silver took two, figuring he could use them to communicate with his team. From his bag, he removed one of the Sig MPX and loaded it before swinging the bag over his shoulder.

On his way out of the vault, he heard footsteps coming from the hall. Two of Tyson's men were moving toward the vault with their assault rifles trained on him. The muzzles of their guns sparked red, and bullets whizzed by him crashing into the cabinet and bench inside the vault. Four thunderous claps followed just microseconds after. He evaded their line of fire and shot three rounds from the MPX as he took cover by the door. He peeked into the hall and saw one man lying stiff on the floor and the other ducking behind a pillar. Silver dodged into the hallway and dropped to his belly, aiming his gun at the pillar. The man stepped out and Silver shot him twice, center mass. The man dropped his weapon and fell to the ground next to his partner. Silver crawled to his feet and used the lever to close the vault's door before heading toward the stairwell. On his way down, he heard a rapid burst of gunfire followed by three single but equally spaced blasts. Downstairs, he saw Semy with her pistol aimed at one of Tyson's men's lifeless bodies.

"Semy!" Silver called out. "You okay?"

"Yes. Thank goodness," she replied. "I was more worried about you."

"I'm fine. Any sign of Landon or Tyson yet?"

"No. I'd just managed to tap into the mainframe when the EMP fried everything."

"Yeah, I was stuck in the elevator when it went off."

"My best guess is that Landon and Tyson, if he's with them, are inside the hangar right now."

"Tyson's with them, all right. I saw him a few moments ago."

"Okay, so what's the plan?" she asked Silver, who was searching through his pack for one of the satellite phones.

"Take this," he handed the phone to Semy. "Since ground communications are down, we can use the satellite..."

"I know how satellite phones work," Semy interrupted him.

"Fine," Silver said, rolling his eyes.

Semy chuckled. "Did you just roll your eyes at me, Leroy?" she said. "These phones will work provided they're configured to authenticate with each other."

"Okay. Well, I guess we'll know soon enough. Here, take this," Silver said, opening his bag and handing her the extra MPX and two magazines. "You go secure the first floor, and I'll head for the hangar."

Semy peered through the gun's sights, inserted a magazine, and pulled back the cocking mechanism. "Got it. Be careful, Silver," she said.

"You too," he replied as they parted ways.

As Silver descended the stairs, he noticed a couple of government-issued vehicles through the windows outside the warehouse's compound. Even without looking at the plates, he knew who they were. After, he spotted Anderson talking to some men and pointing toward the building.

Silver knew he had to contact Anderson before the government took drastic measures to eliminate Tyson. He removed his satellite phone and went to the settings. Making note of the current authentication information, he removed it and entered the new credentials he memorized from his past before dialing a phone number. As the satellite phone rang, Silver looked through the window. He saw Anderson duck into one vehicle and remove a sat phone before placing it to his ear.

"This is Anderson," he said over the line.

"Good thing you still keep that sat phone with you," Silver said.

"Silver? Where have you been?" Anderson yelled over the background noise. "I've been trying to reach you for an hour now."

"Yeah, the phones are down," Silver said. "Plus, I've been a little preoccupied."

"Tyson's resurfaced. He's made his move…"

"I know."

"How'd you know?"

"He and his goons are raiding Kirby's warehouse—where the prototype is," Silver told him. "And I'm inside the building now."

"What's the situation like on the inside?" Anderson asked.

"Well, I don't have eyes on the men, and they took out our comms, but even so we've been able to take out a few of

Tyson's men. I'm pretty sure I can handle the rest, but I'm going to need a favor from you."

"What's that?'

"Make sure the higher-ups don't do anything stupid like bomb the place just to get to Tyson."

"Don't worry, I've got this end covered. And Silver?"

"Yeah?"

"Make sure you kill Tyson this time around. No guilty feelings or excuses this time."

"Roger that," Silver said, ending the call.

When Silver arrived near the hangar, he crouched behind a car and watched while three of Tyson's men roamed the front perimeter. He waited until the men formed a circle and started conversing among themselves before sprinting to the west corner of the hangar. Not wanting to alert those inside of the hangar to his presence, Silver placed his submachine gun on the pavement and shrugged his duffle bag off before setting it next to his gun.

He peeked around the corner and noticed the men were still in a circle. From the bag, Silver removed the two retractable nightsticks, sliding one in the back of his pants and extending the other. Just as he did, the three men broke their huddle. One walked toward the front east corner, another stayed near the center, and the last man paced toward the west edge, where Silver was. When the man was in his line of sight, Silver grabbed him by the collar, yanking him behind the wall and knocking him out with the nightstick. The sound of feet shuffling reached Silver's ears. He peeked and saw the other two men hustling in his direction.

Silver removed the other nightstick and jumped from the corner, striking the hand of the guy closest to him. The man dropped his rifle while the guy behind him slid to a stop and brought his machine gun to bear. Silver flung a nightstick. It connected with the bridge of the guy's nose. The man dropped his gun and reached for his face. Silver then shoved the man closest to him against the wall before kneeing him in the gut and smacking the side of his head with the nightstick. The man spun a half circle and fell to the pavement. The other man arched toward the ground, reaching for his machine gun. Silver ran to him and stomped his hand, then kicked his face. The guy stumbled backward, and as he gained his footing, he drew a long blade from a holster on his waist.

He jabbed the knife at Silver's gut.

Silver back-stepped while striking his opponent's hand with the nightstick and then the top of his head. The man and his knife dropped to the blacktop.

Silver dropped the nightstick and dashed back to his bag. He threw it over his shoulder, picked up his gun, and headed for the hangar's door.

The hangar was about one hundred yards long, and on the far end was a plane. Crates and containers littered the area between him and his objective. Silver spotted legs and feet moving on the opposite side of the aircraft. He continued moving forward, creeping around canisters and bins on his way to the plane. Halfway there, he found Bennett on the floor with two of his men.

Silver knelt and checked Bennett's neck for a pulse, sighing in relief when he found one. There was blood on Bennett's shirt, near his right side. Silver rolled him on his left side and saw where the bullet exited. Only a flesh wound. But Silver knew he had to end this so Bennett could get medical help. At that thought, two of Tyson's goons entered the hangar.

Silver trained his submachine gun on one of them and fired two rounds. One bullet hit the man's shoulder, and the other caught him in the neck. He dropped to the ground and his partner hopped over him.

Silver dove across the floor while the second man directed his rifle at him. Three claps blasted from the goon's gun. Silver slid out of the line of fire. The bullets whistled by him and crashed into the concrete floor as he unloaded four bullets in the man's upper chest.

The man flopped backward and slammed into a pile of crates.

Immediately, metal clanked from the opposite side of the plane. Silver looked under the aircraft. There were crowbars and large wrenches on the floor and feet shuffling. A group of men scurried out. Three reached for their guns, but before they could lift their arms, Silver fired off a burst of rounds. The blasts were deafening. The bullets ripped through the men as their bodies danced and dropped.

Tyson and Landon were standing behind the fallen men. Both shrank back with their hands in front of their faces.

Silver turned the MPX at Landon and pulled the trigger. The gun clicked empty.

*Bummer.*

"It looks like you're out of ammo," Landon said with a smirk on his face.

"But I'm not," Semy said from behind Silver. She held a Beretta M9 in each hand, pointing one at Landon and the other at Tyson.

Dropping the empty submachine gun, Silver removed his 9mm from his holster and cocked it.

"Leroy Silver," Tyson drawled, "you just seem to be all in my business these days."

"Yeah," Silver said, "I made the mistake of not killing you when I had the chance."

"I won't hold that against you," Tyson shrugged. "You probably thought you were doing the right thing."

"Well, I won't make the same mistake twice," Silver stated, pointing his gun at Tyson's forehead.

Tyson smiled, his eyes flicking slightly to Silver's left.

"Semy, nine o'clock!" Silver yelled as one of Tyson's men approached their side.

She fired twice and sent the crony spinning to the pavement. But with the distraction, Landon shot a few rounds in their direction. One bullet hit Semy in her shoulder.

Silver dodged the gunfire and took down Landon with two shots to his kneecaps. Landon dropped his gun, screaming in agony as he clutched his wounds. Silver looked in Tyson's direction and saw the war criminal racing toward the front of the hangar. Silver fired a round at him, but the bullet crashed into a large container that Tyson disappeared behind.

"Missed him," Silver scoffed before walking to Landon and picking up the wounded man's gun. "I would finish you off, but I need you alive," Sliver told him. "Someone has to pay for all this."

He then raced to Semy. "You okay?" he asked.

"Yeah, I'm good," she replied, "Just a minor flesh wound. I'm afraid Tyson got away."

"He won't get far," Silver said, crinkling his nose and shaking his head. "Anderson has the compound surrounded. I'll be right back."

Silver ran outside the hangar, his head on a swivel, but saw no sign of Tyson. He figured the war criminal would head for the garage, grab a car, and try to escape. Silver raced to the main building and took the stairs to the second floor, stopping at the window overlooking the garage. Outside, Tyson was walking toward one of the SUVs, looking over his shoulder every few steps.

The car's engine turned over as Tyson entered on the front passenger side.

*There's no way I'm letting you leave here alive,* Silver thought to himself. He removed the SRS-A2 sniper rifle from his bag and quickly assembled it before raising his 9mm and shooting a round into the window. The glass shattered and he aimed the sniper rifle through the window frame.

The first round hit the driver, and he slumped over the steering wheel. Tyson leaned over and grasped at the wheel, but Silver fired two more shots, hitting him and sending the car crashing into a nearby wall.

Silver made his way down the stairs to the spot where the car crashed. Tyson opened the door, fell to the pavement, and crawled. He was losing a lot of blood and wouldn't last long.

Tyson looked up as Silver approached him. He stopped moving and pulled himself to rest against the car's tire.

"Please, help me," Tyson said in a weak tone. "I can pay double what she's paying you. Just get me out of here, and I'll make you rich," he said, then coughed.

Silver shook his head. "I don't want your money."

"What do you want then? Everyone has a price. Everyone needs something. I can make it happen for you... Like I did for Landon."

"I'm not Landon," Silver grunted, "and the only thing I want is for you to go away, for good. You've caused enough trouble for me and the people in my life."

"Wait...wait," Tyson pleaded, coughing harder. The cough quickly turned into a hack and he choked before his eyes slowly closed.

"I guess I can save that bullet. Would've been a waste anyway," Silver mumbled to himself.

---

The feds made their way into the building to round up the remaining perps. Bennett and Semy were taken to the nearest hospital for immediate medical attention.

"Looks like you had fun here," Anderson said, as Silver walked toward the front of the compound.

"It was okay," Silver shrugged.

"So, I spoke to the higher-ups, and they're relieved that the Tyson situation has been handled."

"Hmm..." Silver grunted. "I didn't do it for them."

"Either way, they want you back. They're impressed with everything that went down here and how you handled the situation. You can have your old job back—with added perks and a raise."

"Nah, I'm good. But I'll take my pension they're holding up."

"Fine," Anderson laughed. "After your performance today, I'm sure they'll be okay with that."

"Thanks, man," Silver said, walking away from his former boss.

"So, what are you going to do now?" Anderson called out.

Silver stopped walking. "Who knows," he said, shrugging. "I might just retire after I get my pension and finally live an honest life," he said, his thoughts drifting to Julia.

"Somehow, I doubt that," Anderson chuckled. "You'd get bored quickly."

"Maybe. But if that happens, I can always continue this freelance thing."

"Sounds like a good idea. Don't be a stranger, Leroy. Call me when you figure out what you want to do."

"Will do." Silver nodded before he turned and continued walking out of the compound.

The first thing he wanted to do was get a cold drink and then call Julia to tell her she could come home. Silver missed seeing the bartender, even though he'd never admit it to her face.

Kirby might want him to keep working for her, but Silver didn't know if he wanted to. Getting his pension would mean he could retire comfortably and live a semi-normal life. But then again, comfortable and normal was not his style.

*I guess we'll just have to see how things turn out.*

# ALOHA & BULLETS

LEROY SILVER'S ADVENTURE CONTINUES

# CHAPTER ONE

WHEN SOMEONE HAS a head start, chasing them on foot can be challenging, especially while wearing a tailored suit and a pair of Stacy Adams. This is what Leroy Silver was pondering as he pursued a lanky, red-haired, freckled face man through the streets of Lower Manhattan. It was just after noon when Silver spotted him in the lobby of the office building where he worked. The freckle-faced young man had been snapping pictures, and since the company didn't allow picture taking, for national security reasons, Silver made his way across the lobby and toward the man to inform him of the company's policy. But when the lanky guy saw him approaching, he jetted out of the building and up the street.

Silver dodged and threaded around pedestrians. "Hey, I just want to talk!" he called to the young man.

The kid just glanced over his shoulder and kept running. He shoved through a crowd and continued across an intersection, but the red crosswalk light indicated he shouldn't have. A white car honked as it sped by, almost hitting him. And before the redhead guy made it to the opposite side, an SUV screeched to a halt, nudging him off balance and sending him flopping to the pavement.

The man crawled to his knees and inspected the now detached lens of the camera that hung around his neck. "Ah man!"

Silver caught a whiff of burnt rubber as he grabbed him by his jacket collar, yanked him off the street, and threw him against the wall. "Who are you?"

"Let go of me!" the young guy said as he pushed against Silver's arms.

Silver put his forearm to the kid's chest, then used his free hand to pat him down. He felt the young man's chest expand and contract and the heat from his exhales breeze across his forearm.

A curvy woman with straight brown hair exited the SUV and walked to them with both hands covering her mouth. "Oh my goodness, are you crazy!" she said to the kid.

Keeping the guy pressed against the wall, Silver turned to face her. "Ma'am please get back in your vehicle," he said, extending his arm between her and redheaded guy.

"This lunatic ran out in the middle of the street."

"I know, I'll take care of it."

"I'm sorry. He was chasing me," the young man said, nodding at Silver.

"Shut up," Silver told him.

"You're not hurt, are you? Because this was your fault," the woman said.

"No, he's not hurt," Silver answered.

"How do you know that?" the lanky man asked.

"I said shut up."

Multiple cars honked. Silver glanced at the street and saw a line of vehicles behind the woman's SUV. "Ms., you have to move your car," he said.

"Okay. You don't look hurt, so I'm leaving. But next time, pay attention to the light," the curvy woman said before walking back to her car.

Silver continued to pat the young man down and found an ID card in his front pocket. *The Big A Tribune* sat in bold print at the top of the card, and at the center was an image of the kid with the name *Bobby Hartley* and the title *Associate Reporter*.

Silver released his captive. "So Bobby, you work for that small newspaper no one ever reads. Question is, why did you run?" he said before tossing the ID card to Bobby.

"I ran because you were chasing me."

"I was only going to tell you that taking pictures in the building's not allowed."

"Well, it doesn't matter now," Bobby said while lifting his busted camera.

"Like the lady said, that's your fault. Now, get out of here."

Bobby scoffed. "Jerk," he said, shaking his head and continuing up the sidewalk.

Silver watched Bobby until the young man disappeared into a crowd of passersby before making the walk back to the office. When he arrived at the front entrance, the doors slid apart and a pale, full-figured man in a security guard uniform stepped out.

"Boss, did you catch him?" the man asked.

"Yeah, I got him, Greg," Silver answered.

Greg glanced behind Silver. "Well, where is he?"

Silver shook his head. "Don't worry about it. He was just a reporter," he said as he walked past Greg and to the doors.

"Wow, you chased him for nothing. You shouldn't be working so hard just before your vacation, boss."

"Tell me about it. Next time, I'm letting you do the chasing."

Silver heard a slapping noise behind him as he entered the lobby, and when he glanced over his shoulder, he saw Greg drumming his belly with his hands.

"I don't know. I've got to get this body chase ready first."

Silver laughed. "We can work on that. I'm taking a break. I'll be in my office."

"Sure thing, boss."

Silver continued across the concrete, polished lobby floor and to the elevator. He pressed the up arrow, and a floral scent struck his nose as the elevator doors opened. The fifth floor was his stop. The west wing of the floor housed I.T. support and surveillance staff, while most of the security team sat in the east wing. Silver headed to the far east wall, passing a few offices and conference rooms on his way. In the corner was a spacious office with large glass windows. Printed on the office door's plaque were the words, *Cush Industries*, and printed below that, *Leroy Silver, Head of Security*. Inside the office, a teal-colored carpet with circular designs covered the floor. The furniture consisted of a desk with an executive chair behind it and two guest chairs in front of it. On the opposite side of the room, a sofa rested against the wall perpendicular to a window with a view that framed most of Manhattan.

Silver plopped into the executive chair and sighed. "That was the most excitement I've had in months," he uttered to himself as his gaze went to a picture on his desk. The picture showed Silver side-hugging a woman with long, curly hair. Her skin had color but was noticeably lighter next to Silver's brown skin. The two had big smiles on their faces and were standing in Central Park. "I wonder how your day is going, Jules."

At that thought, Silver's desk phone rang.

"Cush Industries, Leroy Silver speaking," he answered.

A man chuckled. "I had to hear it for myself," the familiar voice said.

"Matt Anderson, how have you been?"

"Good, but when I heard the great Leroy Silver resorted to the cubicle lifestyle, I couldn't resist calling." Anderson continued laughing.

"Ha-ha. It's honest work, and it keeps me doing something."

"Yeah, but we both know a man with your skillset doesn't belong in an office. I bet you're bored."

Silver exhaled. "To tears. The funny thing is, the boredom is actually draining me."

"You can always come back to the unit."

"No, I'm done working for the government. And like I told you, some orders I just can't follow."

"I know. Just remember you always have a friend here."

"I will."

"Hey, maybe we can get together sometime this weekend and catch up."

"I can't. Jules and I are heading to Hawaii."

"That's right. How long will you be there?"

"We're leaving out early tomorrow, and we'll be back in a week."

"You two have been spending a lot of time together."

"We're just friends."

"Yeah, okay. Well, I think you'll really enjoy that resort, but look, have fun on your trip, and I'll talk to you when you get back."

"Okay man, talk to you later," Silver said, before placing the phone back on the hook.

As he leaned backward in the chair, he heard another

phone ring. This time, it was his personal cell phone. The name *Kirby Cush* displayed on the screen.

"Hello Ms. Cush," he answered.

"Good afternoon, Mr. Silver. How's everything? Still quiet?" Kirby said.

"Well, earlier we had a wannabe reporter in the lobby taking pictures, but other than that, things have been quiet."

"That's great. Quiet is good."

"Kirby, I'm happy you called. I need to talk to you about something."

"Wonderful, because I need to have a word with you too."

"Sure. What is it?"

"It's—it's better if we talk in person. I know you're leaving for your trip tomorrow, so can you cut out early and stop by the mansion on your way home?"

"Yes, ma'am."

"Ma'am?" Kirby laughed. "We had this talk before Leroy," she said, stretching out the syllables of his name. "You don't have to call me ma'am; you're older than I am."

"Just trying to show a little respect."

"I know. That's one of the things I admire about you. But anyway, I'll see you in a little while—oh wait. You had something you wanted to tell me?"

"We'll talk about it when we meet."

"You sure?"

"Yes ma—Yes. Just yes."

Kirby giggled. "Okay, I'll see you then," she said before ending the call.

An hour and a half later, Silver called for a driver to bring one of the company's town cars to the front of the building. He slid into the back seat and instructed the driver to take him to Kirby's home. They arrived at a massive estate surrounded by an enormous gate that made it nearly impossible to see what was on the other side. The driver rang the bell at the gate and looked at the intercom speaker in anticipation, as if he had done it before. Eight seconds passed and nothing happened. The driver rang the bell again, but still no answer.

"They must not hear the bell," he said to Silver.

Silver looked at the driver, then the gate's bell panel. "Hm," he huffed as he exited the car. He circled around the trunk and walked to the panel.

A digital keypad protruded next to the bell button. Silver pressed the number for the code, and a couple seconds later, the gate buzzed open. Silver entered the car, and they drove through and onto a brick driveway. A large mansion sitting on a huge plot of land welcomed them, and at the front entrance, a gold sedan sat parked with the trunk door open. The driver stopped a few yards behind the car and Silver saw the mansion's front door wide open.

"Wait here," he told the driver before exiting the car, removing his Glock 22, and aiming it at the front door of the house. He made it five feet from the door before a petite Asian woman stepped out.

The woman jumped. "Leroy! What are you doing? Trying to scare me to death?"

Silver released a sharp exhale. "Oh, Semy."

"Yes, it's me, Semy," she said, brushing past him and walking to the back of the sedan.

"Sorry," Silver said, as he holstered his gun. "Where's everyone, and why is the door open?"

Semy removed a suitcase and a laptop case from the back before shutting the trunk door. "Everyone is inside, and the door is open because I just got here," she answered as she walked past Silver again.

"Need a hand?" he asked as she passed.

"Nope, got it."

Silver waved at the driver and followed Semy into the house. She sat her bags on the foyer floor.

"Moving in?" Silver said, stepping inside and closing the door behind himself.

Semy brushed her short, straight, black hair behind her ear and sighed as she placed her hands on her hips. "Yep, only for a few days, though. Kirby and I are going to enjoy some girl-time," she said with a smile.

"Oh, you mean like a slumber party? You're telling me the PD gave you time off for that?"

Semy tilted her head and poked her lips. "Do we look like we're twelve, and I'm entitled to my personal leave."

Silver hunched his shoulders.

"Whatever, Leroy," Semy said as she removed her hands from her hips. "For your information, we girls will spend the next few days at the spa, shopping and pampering ourselves."

Footsteps knocked from the opposite side of the foyer. "I'm sorry ma'am, let me get your luggage," the butler said as he approached Silver and Semy.

"Not a problem, I got it," Semy said.

The man picked up her bags. "But I insist; you're a guest." He then turned to Silver and nodded, "Good afternoon, Mr. Silver. Ms. Cush has been expecting you. She's in the kitchen."

Silver returned the nod. "Thanks, Stan."

The butler then faced Semy. "I'll take these to your usual

room," he said before walking past the staircase and toward a hall.

"Usual room?" Silver said. "You might as well move in."

"Shut up," Semy said. "Kirby's my girl. Like a sister to me."

"Well, let me go see what your sista wants."

The two walked across the foyer and to the kitchen. A tall blonde stood at the kitchen island, and standing with her, were a young maid and two security guards. The group wore smiles and laughed.

"No wonder I had to buzz myself through. Half of the staff is in here. Kirby, you approved this?"

The tall blonde looked at Silver with pursed lips. Her eyes were blue with a hint of green. "There you are," she said, walking to where he and Semy stood. "We can talk in my study," she said to Silver. She then turned to Semy and pointed. "You ready, girl?"

Semy pointed back at her. "Oh, I'm ready."

"Let me go handle this business, and we'll get this party started."

The two giggled.

"Oh brother," Silver said, before walking out of the kitchen.

Kirby followed him, and the two walked upstairs and through a set of double doors. They entered a spacious room with tall bookshelves and picture-covered walls. Kirby walked behind a desk at the far end of the room, opened a drawer, and removed an envelope. She handed it to Silver.

"What's this?" he asked.

"Leroy, when you first came to me, it was by high recommendation. And in these past few months, I've witnessed firsthand why that was the case. You are good—no, great at what you do. I trust you and feel my company and I are much safer when you're around. You're an incredible head of security and an even more incredible friend. So, I just wanted to give you something to show my gratitude as your boss and friend."

Silver opened the envelope and saw a check and number with many zeros behind it. "Are you sure? This is a lot of money. You know I'm not hurting; I received a pension from my previous job."

Kirby shook her head as she stepped closer to him. "I'm positive. And I'm not concerned about how your previous employer compensated you. You've earned this for the hard work you've done for Cush Industries."

"Okay, well, I'm not going to argue with the boss," Silver said.

Kirby hugged him. "Thank you for everything you do," she said. "Now, get out of here. You have to get ready for your trip, and Semy and I have a lot to get into."

"You two better behave. I won't be here to bail you out of jail."

Kirby laughed. "Get out of here. Oh wait, you said you wanted to talk to me about something."

Silver looked down and patted the envelope against his palm. "It was nothing," he said, crinkling his nose and shaking his head.

"Okay, get out of here. Enjoy your time off; you deserve it."

## CHAPTER TWO

"YOU CAN DROP me off here," Silver said to the driver.

"Yes, sir," the driver said before veering off the busy street and parking near the curb.

"You don't have to wait for me, I'll catch a cab home."

"You sure?"

"Yep. Thanks for chauffeuring me around today," Silver said as he stepped out of the car and onto a foot-traffic heavy sidewalk.

The driver pulled off and Silver stretched under a dusk-filled sky before directing his attention to a unit with the words *McLarens' Sports Bar* printed above it. Silver smiled as he entered but crinkled his nose at the smell of alcohol and chicken wings. Blaring music stuffed the bar, and every ten seconds, a new customer entered.

He looked behind the bar counter and spotted his favorite bartender and friend, Julia. She was on the opposite side, serving drinks to a group of rowdy men. Silver found a stool and watched as Julia placed a line of shots in front of the men. They downed the drinks, then threw their arms in the air and screamed like they were at a Super Bowl game.

Silver grinned and shook his head before looking at Julia again. She wore a pair of fitted blue jeans and a black long-sleeve button-up shirt with her hair tied back. She looked good. After a few seconds, she looked Silver's way, and a smile grew on her face as she walked to him.

"Why hello there, Mr. Silver," she said.

"I thought you'll be done by now."

"Oh, I am. Just helping out a little, Fridays can get crazy."

Silver nodded and smiled. "So. Are you ready for this?"

Julia's eyes and mouth both widened. "Am I! This trip's all I've been thinking about today, all I've been thinking about this week." She smiled, eyes still wide.

"Yeah, me too."

The counter vibrated as one of the men on the opposite end began slapping the top.

"Another round," he said before looking at the ceiling and howling.

"I have to take care of this pack of wolves, and after, I'll be ready to go, okay?" Julia said.

Silver chuckled. "I'll be here."

"Do you want anything to drink while you wait?"

"Yeah, give me a Roy Rogers."

"Are you serious? Wait, that's right, you're cutting back."

Silver smiled at her.

"One Roy Rogers coming up," she said as she grabbed a bottle from the shelf, walked to the other side of the bar, and filled the shot glasses for the wolves. On her way back, she replaced the bottle and grabbed a glass and a can of Coke. She sat the glass in front of Silver and poured the Coke before reaching for a bottle of grenadine syrup and adding it to the Coke.

"Here you go," she said while adding a straw and stirring

the drink, then pushing the glass closer to him. "It's on the house."

"Thanks."

Julia placed her elbows on the bar top and rested her chin on her palms. "You're welcome," she said, smiling and looking at him.

Silver took a sip. "Not bad."

Julia pushed from the counter. "Not bad," she said as she rolled her eyes.

"No, it's actually pretty good. The best Roy Rogers I've ever had."

Julia slapped the countertop. "That's more like it."

Silver laughed before taking another sip of his drink.

"While you have your drink, I'll go get my things."

He raised his glass to her as she walked away and disappeared through a set of swinging doors. Five minutes later, Silver finished his drink, and Julia walked from behind the bar with a suitcase, a small duffel bag, and her purse. He grabbed the suitcase and rolled it behind himself as he followed her outside.

"I see you're already packed," Silver said.

"I figured we can just go straight to the airport from your house. I know you don't mind me crashing there."

"How do you know? I could be expecting company."

Julia laughed. "You're not, except for me now."

The two walked to the curb to hail a cab, and fifteen minutes later, they were standing in Silver's apartment.

Julia placed her luggage by the door. "Is this new furniture, Lee?" she said with a big smile as she walked to the living room and rubbed the sofa cushion.

"Yeah, I thought it was time."

"You did the decorations yourself?"

"Yep."

"Why didn't I know about this?"

"Because you haven't been here in almost a week."

Julia performed a ballet spin and plopped on the sofa. "Kirby must be paying you well. Wait, you're not giving her any overtime, are you?"

Silver, still standing, chuckled. "I'm ignoring that question, but she did give me a huge bonus today."

"Really?"

"Yeah, between my pension from my previous job, the money I've made working for her, and the bonus I got today, I'm pretty much set with my finances."

"That reminds me, did you tell her?"

"No, not yet."

"Does she at least know about you—you know, being James Bond and all."

"You mean does she know I used to be an assassin for the government. I think she may know something, but I never shared any details."

Julia hunched her shoulders. "Well, what makes you think she knows anything?"

"Kirby may be young, but she's very well connected. When she first asked me about the ten-year gap in my portfolio, I just told her it was classified. But I don't think she would've kept me around this long without doing a little more digging into me and being okay with what she found, so I'm not too concerned about it either way."

Julia rested her elbow on the back of the sofa, tracked her hand through her hair, and massaged the back of her head. "That's fine, but you still should tell her your plans."

"I will. Just haven't gotten around to it."

Julia yawned. "Okay, well, we have to get up early and

I'm hungry. Let's order pizza, my treat. No, better yet, your treat."

Silver smiled. "That's a great idea."

---

Early the next morning, Silver rose from the sofa and stretched before walking to his bedroom and knocking on the door. After a few seconds, he heard movement and a moan from the other side.

"Ahh, is it time to go already?" Julia said.

"Yeah, we need to be at the airport in two hours."

It took them an hour and a half to clean up, dress, get to LaGuardia, go through security, and make it to their gate. Their plane just started boarding when they arrived, and they were among the first to board and take their seats since they were in first class. Julia sat by the window and Silver sat next to her in the aisle seat. The next twenty minutes were noisy, with passengers entering and stowing their luggage and the flight attendants giving directions. Twenty minutes after that, the plane was in the air and the flight attendant served breakfast. It was sausage, eggs, hash browns, toast, fruit, and juice. Silver had orange juice with his breakfast, and Julia had apple juice with hers. The two talked and napped for six hours before landing in Denver.

"The first leg's over," Sliver said as the plane parked at the jetway.

"I don't know if I can handle another six hours, Lee," Julia said.

"Sure you can. Think about the beach and palm trees."

She lifted her chin and raised an eyebrow. "Okay, you're right. I can."

The intercom scratched, and the flight attendant's voice

spoke. "In a few moments the cabin door will open. We ask that you remain seated until the overhead seatbelt light is off. If this is your final destination, we want to thank you for flying with us and wish you a great stay here in Denver, Colorado. And for those who will continue with us to Honolulu, we ask that you remain seated while others deplane. We'll be around shortly to serve refreshments."

A moment later, the flight attendant pulled the cabin door latch until the door thumped and hissed open. A ding permeated the cabin and the clicking of seat belts followed. Over half the passengers stood, gathered their belongings, and herded off the plane and into the jet bridge. When the aisle cleared, Silver stood, stretched, then went to the restroom. On his way back, he found Julia in the aisle, stretching her hands above her head.

"I'm going to the restroom," she said as she slid past him.

Silver nodded and then took his seat.

Shortly after, three people entered the plane. Two were Asian men. Both dressed in jeans and light coats. The first guy had a clean shave and wore his hair tapered, while his partner sported a bald head and goatee. A woman in hand-cuffs walked between the two. She wore jeans with a short-sleeved shirt and had long, dark hair, full lips, and a heart-shaped face. She looked Asian but more Pacific Islander, given her light brown complexion. As the group passed through the aisle, Silver saw a badge and gun on one of the man's hips. *U.S. Marshals.* The three continued up the walkway until they found their seats near the back of the plane.

Julia exited the restroom and walked back to her seat. Silver stood, and she scooted past him to the window.

"Did I miss anything?" Julia asked as she sat.

Silver shook his head. "Nope."

Six and a half hours later, the plane landed at The Daniel K. Inouye International Airport, and Silver and Julia were the first off the aircraft. They threaded through the airport and made it to ground transportation, where they found their shuttle service. Moments later, they climbed into the back seat of a small van and left the airport. Sunlight penetrated through the partly clouded afternoon sky and shone over various bodies of water and mountains in the distance.

"Ahh, it's so beautiful here, Lee," Julia said as she fixated on the passenger side window.

"It's definitely a sight."

"I know you've come here before, but how many times?"

"A few."

"For work?"

Silver shrugged.

"Oh, I get it, it's *classified*," Julia said.

Silver looked at her and smiled.

The van droned down the road a few more miles and palm trees and buildings rolled by as they drove through downtown Honolulu. Silver and Julia continued to take in the sights until the driver turned into a driveway with tall palms on either side. The driver continued until they arrived at the front of a large resort.

"We're here," he said before throwing the van in park, sliding out, and opening the van's trunk.

When Silver exited the shuttle, the driver held his luggage, which was only a small duffel bag.

"That's mine, I'll carry it," Silver said to the driver as he grabbed the bag.

"I see you like to pack light," the driver said.

"Take only what you need; more than that is just extra weight."

"I hear that, makes my job a lot easier at least. I'll get the rest from the back."

When Julia stepped out of the van, she walked with Silver into the resort while the driver followed closely behind with her luggage. They went to the receptionist desk, tipped the shuttle driver, checked in, then took the elevator upstairs to their adjoining rooms. Both had their own bathroom, living area, and bed. Silver and Julia figured it was best for them to have a little privacy. At least that's what they agreed on.

Silver tossed his bag on the bed before walking to the balcony window and sliding the blinds open. Light raced in, warming his face, and a view spanning from the beach and out into the ocean came into sight. He took it all in for a moment before hearing a knock from the room's adjoining door. Julia stood on the other side with a big smile.

"I love it here!" she said while brushing past him and into his room. "The floors are marble, I have a king-size bed, a rain shower, and a jacuzzi. What's in your bathroom?" she asked as she darted toward his bathroom.

"The same as your room."

While Julia was in Silver's bathroom, he took a seat on the couch in the living area.

"Oh, yours has the same setup as mine," Julia said from the bathroom.

"Yeah, I told you that."

She walked into the living room. "Oh wow, look at that view," she said, continuing toward the balcony window. "This is amazing, Lee!"

Silver watched as she peered out the balcony window and swayed from side to side like a cheerful kid looking outside at falling snow on Christmas morning. She remained that way for thirty seconds before skipping across the marble floor to his bed and diving onto it. She lay on her side with her elbow pressed into the bed and her head resting in her palm.

Silver stood and walked to her.

"So, what do you want to do first?" she asked.

"We can do whatever you like."

Julia stared at him for a moment before sitting up and standing. "Thank you so much for this," she said, hugging him. "I've pretty much never taken a true vacation and really needed this."

Silver hugged her back. "I have to take care of my favorite bartender, especially since you've always been there for me when I've needed it."

She squeezed him harder, and after a long moment, the two slowly loosened their embrace but still held one another. They looked into each other's eyes and both gradually leaned in to kissing distance.

A loud thump came from the side of the bed. They released each other and saw Silver's bag on the floor.

"Sorry, I must've knocked it to the edge when I jumped on your bed," Julia said.

They laughed.

"So, let's get out of here and get this vacation rolling," Silver said.

"Yes! Let's start with walking on the beach and spending some time by the pool."

"Sounds good to me."

Twenty minutes later, they were on the beach, walking along the coastline. Silver had changed into shorts and a white t-shirt, and Julia wore a gold-colored swimsuit with a laced white shawl tied around her waist. They trekked across the soft, tan-colored sand in flip-flops as the warm water brushed over their feet and the cool breeze wafted across their faces. People lined the beach. Some lay on towels, some on a beach chair, while others played in and on the sand.

Julia stopped and looked at the horizon.

Silver followed her gaze beyond the swimmers, surfers, canoes, and sailboats. "Quite the sight, huh?"

"Yes, it's absolutely beautiful."

They continued up the beach and walked for over an hour before heading to the pool and having a few virgin daiquiris and pina coladas. While there, the server told them about a restaurant that served the best steak and seafood in town, so they went upstairs, changed clothes, and walked to the restaurant. Silver enjoyed the most tender steak he had in a long time, and Julia raved about the lobster. They ate, talked, and laughed for two hours before heading back to the resort. It was dark when they entered the lobby.

Julia sighed. "That was so much fun," she said as they approached the elevators.

"It was, but I think all the traveling and walking is catching up with me," Silver said before pressing the up arrow.

"Yeah, I'm ready for bed."

When they entered the elevator, Silver jabbed their floor number, but before the doors could close, a familiar man entered. The U.S. Marshal with the tapered haircut. He carried a large brown bag with grease stains at the bottom and a beverage holder with three Styrofoam cups.

"Floor?" Silver asked him.

The man tilted his head and looked at the elevator's control panel. "That's it."

Silver eased toward the back of the elevator with Julia and kept his eye on the guy's back.

"I don't know about you, but I'm going to soak in the jacuzzi," she said.

"I think I'll do the same," Silver said, still looking at the guy.

"Tomorrow we should take a tour."

"Uh huh."

Julia turned to Silver. "Lee, are you even listening to me?"

He looked at her with wrinkles across his forehead. "Of course I am."

The man glanced over his shoulder at them. Shortly after, the elevator dinged, and the doors slid apart. The man stepped out. Silver and Julia followed him all the way to their rooms. While Julia removed her keycard and fiddled with her door, Silver watched the man go to a room at the end of the hall and knock on the door.

Julia pushed her door open. "I'm going to figure out how to work the jacuzzi, then I may be over to bother you, okay?"

Silver didn't answer; he just kept his eyes on the guy.

"Did you hear me?" Julia asked, pivoting toward Silver's gaze.

By that time, the door opened, and the man walked inside.

Julia faced Silver again. "What are you doing?" she asked with a slight chuckle.

"Nothing, I just remember seeing that guy on our plane, that's all."

"Oh, really. Well, it's not uncommon, so did you hear what I say?"

"Yeah, you'll be over to bother me," Silver said, grinning as he did.

"Whatever," Julia said before stepping inside her room and sticking her tongue out at him.

Silver rolled his eyes as the door shut in front of him. He glanced down the hall at the room the man entered. "Probably nothing. I'm here to relax," he said to himself before entering his own room.

# CHAPTER THREE

THE NEXT MORNING, Silver woke to knocking from the adjoining door. He opened it to find Julia standing on the other side. She wore a heather-gray t-shirt, twisted into a knot at the bottom, white capri pants, and gray Adidas with white stripes.

"Why are you knocking?" Silver said, as he turned and walked toward the bathroom. "The door's unlocked."

"I didn't want to walk in while you were in your birthday suit," Julia said.

Silver entered the bathroom and washed his face. When he came out, Julia was looking outside through the balcony window.

"I see you're already dressed," he said.

She turned from the window. "Yep. I figured we can get an early start, maybe have some breakfast first."

"Sounds good," Silver replied, as he removed a pair of blue jeans and a polo shirt from his bag.

"Okay," Julia said, before walking to the adjoining door. "I'm going to grab my things while you get ready."

Twenty minutes later, they were in a buffet line at one of

the resort's restaurants. Silver filled his plate, grabbed a bottle of orange juice, and found a place for them to sit. Julia found him a couple of minutes after and set her plate on the table.

"I'll be back, have to run to the restroom," she said.

Silver nodded, chewed his breakfast, and watched as Julia dodged around a few tables before disappearing down a hall. Halfway through his next bite, he noticed two men enter the restaurant. The U.S. Marshals he saw the day before, but they weren't wearing their badges today. The bald one with the goatee held the back of his head, wide eyes, and looking from side to side while his clean shaved partner scanned the room with his mouth gaped. Silver kept his eyes on them as they threaded through the dining area. He wanted to ignore them; he wanted to finish his breakfast and enjoy his time with Julia, but he didn't like being in the dark with a potentially dangerous situation.

"Lost something?" he asked as the two men approached his table.

The bald guy stopped and gave Silver a stare as if he didn't see him sitting there. "I'm looking for a colleague," the man said while reaching into his pocket and removing his phone. He tapped and swiped at it before turning the screen to Silver. "Have you seen this woman?" he asked.

It was a picture of the woman who traveled with them on the plane.

"Who are you?"

"Just a local looking for my colleague."

Silver looked at the gun on the man's hip. "Are you a cop?" he asked.

The man followed his gaze. "Oh no, but I have a permit for this. So, have you seen her?"

Silver took another bite of his food. "I have."

"You have?" the man said before waving to his partner. "Where?"

"On the plane yesterday with you, but I haven't seen her since."

The man scoffed. "Don't waste my time," he said, placing the phone back inside his pocket.

At that moment, the guy with the tapered haircut walked to his bald partner. "What?" he asked.

The bald man shook his head. "Nothing. Let's go."

Silver watched as the two men left the same way they entered. A couple of minutes later, Julia made her way to the table and sat across from him.

"Wow, you just about cleared your plate," she said.

"Yep," Silver replied.

"So, did I miss anything?"

"Nope—well, there is something."

Julia's forehead wrinkled, and she leaned toward Silver with her elbow on the table and her chin in her palm.

"I don't mean to ruin our vacation," Silver said, "but yesterday on the plane, there were two men—"

"You're talking about the men that were with that woman?"

Silver raised an eyebrow. "You noticed them?"

"Yeah, they were sitting near the back of the plane. Don't look so surprised; you're the one always telling me to mind my surroundings."

"No, I'm just shocked you listened to me."

They both chuckled.

"Okay, so what about them?" Julia asked.

"Well, they're staying here."

"They are?"

"You didn't notice the man in the elevator last night?"

"No, I guess I missed that."

"Looks like we have to hone those observation skills."

Julia tilted her head and poked her lip at him.

"But anyway, the two men came in here while you were in the restroom. They were looking for the woman."

"Really?"

"Yeah. It may not be a big deal, but something is going on. Just wanted to make sure you were aware because the two guys are carrying guns."

"Guns? I didn't realize that."

"Um-hum, so if you see them or the woman, stand clear."

"What do you think? I'll go introduce myself to them?" Julia said, as she took the first bite of her breakfast.

"I do recall telling you to stay away from someone before, and you didn't listen. Remember? You had to get out of town."

"That was before I knew you were a secret agent man."

"Right," Silver said, before taking a swig of his orange juice.

"Hey. Do you think we should let the resort's security staff know?"

Silver shrugged. "It won't hurt. That way, it's in the hands of the authorities, and we can enjoy our trip."

They finished their breakfast and made their way to the receptionist in the lobby.

"Good morning, how can I help you?" the young lady at the counter said.

"Good morning. Is there someone from security we can talk to?" Silver asked.

"Is there an issue?"

"I hope not. Just wanted to make them aware of a situation."

"Okay, one moment," she said before entering a room behind the counter.

Julia sighed. "Hopefully this doesn't take too long. I have an exciting day planned."

Silver looked at her and smiled.

A minute later, the receptionist returned. "Someone with security will be down in a few minutes, sir," she said.

Silver nodded. "Appreciate it," he said.

"My pleasure, sir."

Silver then turned to Julia, "While we're waiting for them, I'm going to the bathroom."

"Alrighty, I'll be here, waiting," she said.

Silver went to the restroom and was back in the lobby within four minutes. He saw the receptionist standing next to a man in a black polo shirt and dark khaki green cargo pants with a Ruger LC9 holstered on his hip, but he didn't see Julia.

"This is one of our on-duty officers," the young lady said as Silver approached.

"Hello sir, I understand you had some concerns you wanted to discuss," the man said.

"Yeah," Silver said, while scanning the moderately crowded lobby for Julia. "Where's the woman I was with earlier..." he asked the receptionist as he spotted Julia standing outside near the front entrance.

He stepped in that direction, and while squinting at the glass doors, he saw Julia talking to someone. *The woman from the plane*. Silver increased his walking speed, and as he did, he heard the security officer stepping behind him.

"Sir, sir," the officer called.

Continuing toward the front entrance, Silver glanced back at the officer. When he returned his sights to the front entrance, he saw the two men from the plane hustling out the door and toward the women. Silver sprinted through the lobby, with the security officer following him. As Silver exited the front door, the man with the goatee raised his pistol toward Julia and the Asian woman.

Silver shoulder-butted him, causing the bald man to drop his gun and stumble into his partner. Before the gun could settle on the pavement, Silver scooped it up and aimed it at the two men.

"What do you think you're doing?" he asked them.

Neither of the two men answered, just stood with their arms raised. Julia and the woman with the heart-shaped face watched intently, with gaping mouths and the white of their eyes exposed. Hotel guests and passersby gasped at the sight.

Silver took a step toward the men and said, "Who are—"

"Drop the weapon," the security officer interrupted, with his gun trained on Silver.

Silver watched the officer from his peripheral but kept his gun on the bald man and his clean shaved partner. "These are the two you want to aim your gun at," Silver said to the officer.

"I won't ask again."

Julia and the woman took cover behind a taxicab at the curb, while pedestrians scattered from the area.

Silver looked at the officer, held the gun by the trigger guard with one finger, opened his arms, knelt to the ground, and slid the gun from his finger to the pavement. He then stood with his arms raised and shrugged at the officer.

The security officer kept his gun on Silver. "Good, now kick it over."

As Silver moved his leg to do as the officer asked, he saw the man with the clean shave and tapered hair lifting his own pistol in the security officer's direction.

"Get down!" Silver yelled while diving at guard.

A roaring boom popped through the air, and glass shattered as Silver and the officer crashed through the doors. Silver felt pieces of glass rain down on his back as he and the officer hit the lobby's floor. More people screamed and ran from the lobby and front entrance. Julia and the woman entered the taxicab. The Asian woman jumped in the driver's seat and Julia entered through the back driver's side.

The bald guy picked up his gun. "Let's get her," he said to his partner.

The officer moaned.

Silver inspected his body and saw where the bullet entered his left shoulder.

"You're lucky," Silver told him.

"I don't feel lucky," the officer said.

"Just keep pressure on your shoulder until the medics arrive."

Screeching and gunfire flowed through the air. The cab raced around the resort's driveway and headed for the exit. The two men commandeered a small delivery truck parked near the curb and gave chase.

"You don't mind, do you?" Silver asked the security officer as he picked up the officer's Ruger LC9 and dashed outside into smoke and the scent of burnt rubber.

He ran after the truck and hopped on the back bumper as it slowed to make a right turn onto a six-lane highway. He then braced himself by holding the vertical metal rod of the right-side cargo door. The truck rocked and swayed as it droned down the road. Silver tucked the Ruger in his back waistband and straddled to the left side of the truck. The wind struck his face as he peeked around the corner and saw the taxicab twelve yards ahead. Cars honked as the delivery truck zipped past and crossed in and out of lanes.

Grabbing the outside frame of the door with his free hand and tightening his grip on the metal rod with his other, Silver used his feet and shimmied himself to the roof of the cargo trunk. He lay on his belly and crawled toward the front of the truck as the wind pulled at his shirt. When he was halfway to the truck's cabin, the vehicle jerked to the left, and a loud thump followed. The momentum of the truck slid Silver in that direction and over the edge. With the left side of his body hanging over the edge, he looked down and saw a large dent in the taxicab's front passenger door. In the back seat, Julia sat crouched with her arms covering her head, while the woman driving leaned toward the windshield with both hands on the wheel.

Silver pulled himself back on the delivery truck's roof and snailed his way toward the cabin. Traffic thinned, and the palm trees and buildings rolling by on either side were soon replaced by forestry, large bodies of water, and mountains in the distance. Gripping the edge of the cabin's roof and peeking into the driver's side, Silver thrust his left arm through the half-opened window and grabbed the clean shaved man's throat.

"Pull over!" he yelled.

The man took one hand off the wheel and clasped Silver's arm. "G—get off me," he said, struggling to break Silver's grip.

The truck weaved across the highway, and as Silver felt his body sliding toward the edge again, he released his hold on the man's throat and grasped the inside window frame instead. A car driving in the opposite direction laid on its horn until the delivery truck veered onto the right side of the road.

Silver glanced down and saw the cab right next to the truck, and before he could fully adjust his body on the roof, a blast roared from inside the truck's cabin. He quickly released his grip and slid back toward the trunk as two large bullet holes ripped through the cabin's roof. Holding the front brim of the trunk and removing the Ruger, Silver fired three rounds through the cabin's roof. The truck skidded to the left. Silver tucked the Ruger back inside his pants, held tight with both hands, and watched the taxicab screech to a halt as the delivery truck cut it off and stopped in front of it.

Silver climbed down on the driver's side and lurked toward the front. The door swung open and the man with the tapered haircut hopped out from behind the wheel. The moment the clean-shaved man's feet hit the ground, Silver delivered a punch to his jaw. The guy spun, hit the open door, and then fell to the pavement. Silver removed the Ruger and aimed it at the door before jumping inside the cabin. On the passenger side, the bald guy sat, holding his bleeding shoulder. He eyed Silver, then reached for his gun in the middle of the seat. Silver beat him to it, snatching the gun, ejecting the magazine, then tossing the gun out the door.

The injured man chuckled. "You're a dead man," he said. "Do you know who we work for?"

"No, and I get the feeling you're not going to tell me either, huh?" Silver said.

"That's right, I'm not telling you—"

Silver elbowed the man in the head near his temple. The guy slumped over, knocked out.

"You don't have to tell me now; sleep on it," Silver said as he hopped out of the truck.

By that time, traffic had bottlenecked. Some vehicles stopped and looked at the scene, while others slowed just long enough to thread through and continue on their way. Ignoring the honking horns and fussing drivers, Silver walked to Julia, who stood with the other woman near the hood of the cab.

"You couldn't help yourself, could you?" he said.

Julia shrugged. "What are you talking about?"

Silver pointed at the Asian woman. "Her. I told you to stay away."

"It's not what you think."

"Really? Because it looks like you got involved after I told you to stand clear, and I almost killed myself trying to save you."

"First, you're not my dad, and no one told you to jump on the roof of a truck like Spiderman. Second, she was escaping from those men. She said they were going to hurt her."

"Ah, okay. Thank you for clearing that up. The strange woman says it's okay, so it's okay. There's no chance she could be lying, right?"

"Hey, I can hear you; I'm right over here," the woman said.

Julia scoffed before folding her arms and shaking her head. "I forget you can be over the top sometimes," she said to Silver. "And she has a name, Alleen."

"Oh really? I'm sorry I didn't catch it. I was too busy hanging from the back of a truck," Silver said as he pointed at the delivery truck.

"Excuse me," Alleen said.

Julia ignored her. "You didn't even ask if I was okay," she said to Silver. "You just came over and ridiculed me without getting the whole story."

"We need to go," Alleen said.

"I know you, so I know how the story went," Silver told Julia before turning his attention to Alleen.

"Maybe you don't know me as well as you think," Julia said back to him.

Silver followed Alleen's gaze and saw two black SUVs approaching the delivery truck. "We'll finish this later, but we need to go," he said.

"Where are we going to go?" Julia asked. "We're surrounded by jungle, and the cab is blocked in."

"Follow me," Alleen said before jogging to the edge of the road. She climbed over the guardrail and waved at Silver and Julia. "C'mon."

"What should we do?" Julia asked Silver.

"We're in it now. Let's go," Silver said, placing his hand on Julia's back and guiding her to where Alleen stood. Once he helped Julia over the guardrail, Silver glanced back at the SUVs and saw a group of men armed with assault rifles exiting the vehicles. They didn't look his way, just surrounded the delivery truck, and as they did, a man with shades exited one of the SUVs. His suit was a perfect fit for his athletic built, and his slicked back, salt-and-pepper hair matched the color of his full beard.

Silver stared at the man for a moment before hearing Julia and Alleen's voices.

"We have to go now," Alleen said.

"Lee, let's go," Julia said.

Silver jumped over the guardrail, and the group hiked down a grassy incline, then into the woods.

I hope you enjoyed diving into the world of Leroy Silver—a realm brimming with assassins, explosive gunfights, thrilling car chases, and high-octane action around every corner.

It's challenging to pinpoint a single source of inspiration for Silver because he just came to life as the words flowed onto the page. Unlike Orlando Black, Silver operates alongside a lively cast of recurring characters, reminiscent of one of my favorite authors, Stephen J. Cannell's The A-Team. There's also a hint of Magnum P.I. and The Fall Guy in his adventures. Sometimes, Silver's escapades even evoke memories of Burn Notice.

These shows represent the kind of entertainment I grew up with—clean, witty, gripping fun that kept you on the edge of your seat. They didn't just entertain; they inspired and encouraged viewers, showcasing characters who defied all odds for the greater good.

My wish for this series and all my books is to entertain, inspire, and encourage you along your journey. I hope this story has done just that for you. If you enjoyed it, please consider leaving a review at the store where you purchased the book.

If anything in this letter resonates with you, I'd love to hear from you and learn more about your experiences. Feel free to reach out.

Thank you for allowing me and Leroy Silver into your life.

Alex Cage

connect@alexcage.com

www.alexcage.com

# ALSO BY ALEX CAGE

More books by Alex Cage. Have you read them all? Grab your next adventure today!

**Leroy Silver Series**

Contracts & Bullets

Aloha & Bullets

Politics Thieves & Bullets

**Orlando Black Series**

Carolina Dance

Bayside Boom

Bet on Black

Get the latest releases and exclusive giveaways, sign up to the Alex Cage Reader List.

www.AlexCage.com/signup

# JOIN THE READER'S LIST

Get the latest releases and exclusive giveaways - sign up to the Alex Cage Reader List:

www.AlexCage.com/signup

# ABOUT THE AUTHOR

Alex Cage is a thriller author and passionate wordsmith who loves to blend his fascination with martial arts and travel with high-octane action and explosive adventures. He enjoys nothing more than entertaining his readers with death-defying missions, larger-than-life characters, and suspenseful stories that always find a way to keep you on your toes.

As the author of nearly a dozen titles, including the Orlando Black series and the Leroy Silver series, Alex combines his obsession for thrillers with a sprinkling of fantasy and sci-fi, so that readers will always find something to capture their imagination. He currently resides in North Carolina. When not writing his next novel, you can find him reading and practicing martial arts.

Find out more about Alex Cage (and get a free read):

www.alexcage.com
connect@alexcage.com

ALEX CAGE
CLEAN FAST-PACED ACTION THRILLERS